shooting stars everywhere

shooting stars everywhere

martina wildner

TRANSLATED FROM THE GERMAN BY JAMES SKOFIELD

DELACORTE PRESS

Published by
Delacorte Press
an imprint of
Random House Children's Books
a division of Random House, Inc.
New York

Translation copyright © 2006 by James Skofield
Originally published in German under the title *Jede Menge Sternschnuppen*
copyright © 2003 by Beltz & Gelberg in der Verlagsgruppe Beltz, Weinheim Basel Berlin,
Germany. All rights reserved.
Jacket photograph copyright © 2006 by Andy Whale © Tony Stone / Getty Images

The trademark Delacorte Press is registered in the
U.S. Patent and Trademark Office and in other countries.

Visit us on the Web! www.randomhouse.com/teens

Educators and librarians, for a variety of teaching tools,
visit us at www.randomhouse.com/teachers

Library of Congress Cataloging-in-Publication Data
Wildner, Martina.
Shooting stars everywhere / Martina Wildner ; translated from the German by James
Skofield.
p. cm.
Summary: Thirteen-year-old Victor keeps a journal about the mysterious letters that
began arriving on his birthday, his fear of the high diving board, confusion over his
divorced parents' relationship, and an assertive girl he calls D.
ISBN 0-385-73250-3 (trade) — ISBN 0-385-90272-7 (glb)
[1. Diving—Fiction. 2. Interpersonal relations—Fiction. 3. Letters—Fiction. 4. Family
life—Germany—Fiction. 5. Diaries—Fiction. 6. Germany—Fiction. 7. Mystery and
detective stories.] I. Skofield, James. II. Title.
PZ7. W6466Sh 2006
[Fic]—dc22
2005009311

The text of this book is set in 12-point Myriad Roman.

Book design by Kenny Holcomb

Printed in the United States of America

March 2006

10 9 8 7 6 5 4 3 2 1

BVG

My thanks to Michael, Stefanie, Dorothee,
Joachim, Anne-Dore, Julia, and the
New Society for Literature, Berlin

—M.W.

WEDNESDAY, JULY 24

These are the dog days. The dog days are named after the Dog Star, Sirius, which rises with the sun every July twenty-third. July twenty-third is my birthday.

Other than that, there isn't much to say about my thirteenth birthday. Instead of a skateboard, I got a journal, and instead of birthday cards, there was a letter in the mailbox. Actually, I don't know whether or not it was for me, since there was nothing written on the envelope. It was a letter from no one to no one. I don't know why I opened it; I guess I thought since it was my birthday, it must be for me. Maybe it was a letter from Mom?

> the red animal is dead
> beware of strangers
> and dark clouds of dust
> for they will swallow you up
> just like everyone here
>)x(

Definitely not a letter from Mom. Mom wouldn't send me a birthday death threat. Maybe the letter was a stupid joke from someone in my class. I read in the newspaper recently that it's a new school fad to totally beat up any kids having a birthday. It's lucky my birthday usually falls during vacation.

This dumb journal. How did Dad ever arrive at the lame idea of giving me an empty book? Maybe because empty books are cheaper than full ones. Dad sometimes gets strange ideas. Only girls write in journals! Still, the cover is sort of cool—it's actually a shiny, 3-D silver pattern.

It's hot as blazes—the thermometer on the balcony has already hit almost seventy-eight degrees. I go into the kitchen to get myself something to drink. The Coke is flat, because the bottle was left standing in the refrigerator with the cap off. And besides, it isn't even real Coke. Ugh. Fake Coke with no bubbles!

I think today I could probably get annoyed at just about anything, although getting that way is stupid. But it really is difficult not to get upset when you think that the most boring time of the year lies ahead of me: six weeks of summer vacation stuck in the city.

I must really be bored; I'm writing in the journal! Otherwise, I just wouldn't bother.

Dad's left his half-eaten baloney sandwich on the kitchen table. That means he got home late from driving his taxi. When he gets home late, he always makes himself a baloney sandwich before he goes to bed. But I've never understood why he makes himself a whole sandwich when he ends up eating only half of it. And the next morning, it's left for me to get rid of, because the baloney begins to smell. Especially in this heat.

In the meantime, the temperature has climbed to eighty-three, and it's still early. Going swimming would be a good idea.

Kaiser Wilhelm got the baloney sandwich. He was downstairs in the yard. He often spends time down there, hanging out and pooping. Kaiser Wilhelm was very happy about the baloney sandwich. He wagged his tail. Arnold should really take him for walks more often. That way, the dog wouldn't be so fat. Cocker spaniels actually tend to get fat. Arnold says he's got no time, because he has to work so much. He's trained the dog to go down to the yard from the fourth floor all by himself. When it's time for Kaiser Wilhelm to come back upstairs, Arnold whistles out the window for him. As far as dog grooming goes, Arnold is really awfully lazy. That's why that red coat of his dog's is always matted.

Down on the ground floor, I also encountered our neighbor, Mrs. von Grützow. "Goodbye, Fictor," she said as she was locking her door. PSYCHOLOGICAL CONSULTATIONS FOR CHILDREN AND TEENAGERS. GUIDANCE COUNSELING, it says on the plaque outside her door. But she's closed during summer vacation.

My name's Victor, I thought. I always think that when she calls me Fictor, but I've never said it out loud.

Just after Mrs. von Grützow, I ran into the mailman. He had a little package for me. It was from Mom. I unwrapped it while I was still downstairs. I'm now the proud owner of a superexact digital watch. It's waterproof to two-hundred feet. It's now exactly 9:33 a.m. An almost-on-time present from Mom is already something of a rarity.

* * *

3

At the swimming pool, I spread out my towel not far from the diving tower. I'm wearing the digital watch and I've brought the journal with me, so I can write everything down and maybe become the most boring writer in history. Time is especially boring. It's 10:43 a.m. Luckily, no one can see me writing, because I'm alone. Everyone else is off traveling. To America or wherever. I'd like to visit America too, but Dad says there's no chance of going.

For the time of day, the swimming pool's pretty empty, and only the 3- and 7.5-meter diving platforms are open. The 5- and 10-meter platforms are closed. Today, I at least have to jump off the 7.5-meter platform. *I have to.* All my buddies have been jumping off it and the 10-meter, even, for years. I'm the only one who hasn't. I haven't even jumped off the 3-meter. I just keep standing there like an idiot. Besides that, there's that miserable bet. Lukas, that jerk, who's now traveling all over the United States, said to me, "Bet ya by the time I get back from vacation, you *still* won't have dared to jump" and I said, "A bet, huh?" and he said, "Okay. If you don't jump, you have to kiss Saskia. Using your tongue. In front of everybody."

I *can't* lose that bet. Saskia is a nightmare. Her breath stinks so badly you can smell it from five yards away. But the worst thing about Saskia isn't her bad breath; it's the fact that she's a full head taller than I am and has so far managed to beat up any boy who's messed with her. At best, I'd escape with a black eye. Horrible. I've got to jump from the 10-meter platform!

Even from the 7.5-meter platform it looks like you're up damn high, especially when you consider you've got

4

another 1.5 meters to factor in due to your own height. And when you add to that the 4.8 meters of water to the bottom of the pool, it's no wonder you don't dare jump. That's why I'm here at the pool this morning. There aren't so many people here, and there's time to stand at the top, get up your nerve, and peer over the edge without looking like a total idiot. In the afternoons, there's a crowd up on the diving tower, and you've got to look cool.

I'm going to swim now. Water makes everyone happy. I've yet to see an unhappy person in the pool. A couple are splashing, and everyone's laughing. It must have to do with the fact that we all spend a while as fish in our mothers' wombs. That's what Dad said when he showed me the scar from his throat operation and said, "That was my gill."

But maybe the swimming pool will soon see an unhappy person, and that'll be me; if I haven't jumped off the 7.5-meter platform, I mean.

The other thing I like about the swimming pool is the girls. You're able to see girls at the pool like nowhere else. I don't entirely understand girls. For instance, I don't get why they almost never actually go swimming. And hardly ever dive from the platforms. Maybe ten girls a day do, at most. I think they don't like the water and are afraid that if they jump they'll lose their bikinis. One-piece bathing suits would be better for jumping, but one-piece suits, I've observed, seem to be over.

I've just made a fool of myself and in front of a girl, no less. I'd been writing how no girls jump off the platforms or wear one-piece bathing suits, when who should be standing up on the 7.5-meter platform wearing a one-piece suit? And then making the most beautiful dive I've ever seen? A girl.

Nobody was on the tower—only the girl and I. It was a bit breezy up there—breezier than on the ground, at any rate. It seemed like a storm to me—one that would soon blow me off the platform. From up there, everything seemed very tiny—even the lifeguard, who otherwise seems like a real brute.

Anyway—I was standing up there and she was standing up there. I was in front; she was a bit behind me. I was looking down. 13.8 meters, when you add everything up. "You're thinking about it too much," the girl said from behind me. I was really taken by surprise. Then she said, "You've never been off it, have you?"

"Yeah, yeah," I lied. "I'm only looking."

"If you're not going to jump now, can I go ahead of you?"

"Be my guest." I was happy to be rid of her.

The girl had on a turquoise one-piece bathing suit—as turquoise as the water. No, wait—the water isn't turquoise. That's the tiles. Well, it doesn't matter.

She dove in with hardly a splash.

And of course she soon climbed back up again. "You're still up here," she said. "You still haven't jumped. I can tell." The *witch*. As if it were any of her business!

"You know, what you're doing is useless. You won't get anywhere by just staring."

"So what should I do?"

"Climb down."

"What?"

"Climb down and try again later. Just climb back up, walk forward, and jump. Don't think about it. It won't hurt you."

What a *witch*! Take the ladder down! So that everyone could see—I chickened out?

"Believe me. It was that way for me, too."

I didn't believe her. On the other hand . . . there must have been a first time for her, too.

I climbed down. *Climbed.* But I didn't go back up. I really am a loser. Even though my name is still Victor.

An empty book like this is really not such a dumb idea. Books that are full are already completely arranged. The only thing you can decide about them is when you will start or stop reading them. With an empty book, you get to arrange everything yourself. And you can write things in them you'd never tell anyone. That stuff about the 7.5-meter platform, for example. I couldn't tell anyone that. And that a girl made a fool out of me. I can barely admit that to myself. And that the girl is kind of cute. She has long red hair that sticks to her back. And even a little bit of a bosom. But I shouldn't be saying "bosom." In my class, you've got to say "tits." Anyone who says "bosom" is a loser or a biology teacher.

I'm looking around me at the swimming pool. The girl has gone. There's not a trace of turquoise bathing suit anywhere in sight.

Now it's boring here and this empty book is bugging me. Well, that's another thing about an empty book. If nothing occurs to you, you just stare at the blank pages. I'm going home.

Wait. First, I've got to have a look at the thermometer. It's located under the big swimming pool clock. Ninety degrees. Temperatures are fascinating. Why does the sun shine some days and it's only seventy-six, but the very next day it's ninety? In the same month, sometimes even in the very same week? With the same sun. When I was little, I used to think maybe someone was switching the sun around on the sly. Now I know it has to do with air masses. Whether the air masses are warm or cold. But why is one front cold and another one warm? In the same month, in the same week, and with the same sun? Okay, now I'm really leaving.

At exactly 2:03 p.m., I unlock our front door. A note's hanging on the front of it: "Won't be here today. Don't be mad at me!" Mischka's handwriting. I'm not mad at her at all. On the contrary. As far as I'm concerned, she never needs to be here. But she feels she should stop by and bring us a hot meal at least once a week.

Dad is still sleeping. I've made coffee for him. The coffeemaker takes longer each day to get going, because it's all gunked up. I take the chewy bread, jam, and margarine I bought at the supermarket out of the plastic bag. There wasn't money to buy more than that in the tin canister where Dad always dumps his spare change. Maybe I'll switch on the tube. Eating and watching TV at the same time is the best. That's the advantage of having a TV in the kitchen.

I veg out for two hours and watch a program on the pyramids. A scientist is explaining that the pyramids at

Giza were laid out exactly like the stars in Orion's Belt, and that they had been planned that way in 10,500 B.C. The plans and calculations for them were brought by aliens. Orion's a constellation, and you don't see it in the summertime. Orion isn't all that distant from Sirius.

Suddenly, Dad comes shuffling in. His face is rumpled.

"Ah, Victor, whatever would I do without you," he sighs, and helps himself to coffee. "You'd have to make your own coffee," I answer. That's the way our conversation starts almost every day. "What unscientific claptrap is that?" Dad asks, looking warily at the TV. And then he says, "Actually, I wanted to get up earlier today. Tomorrow, can you wake me up by noon?" Dad's often said this, and I've often tried to wake him, but when I do, he just rolls over and grunts, "A little longer . . . Is the coffee ready?" Then I bring him his coffee, but he's already gone back to sleep and the coffee gets cold. Then he curses because the coffee is cold. Lately I've taken to cursing, since he won't make his own coffee. "Oh, Victor, don't be so hard on me," he'll respond while stroking my head. "Just don't be a taxicab driver." Dad says that at least three times a week. "And don't believe that alien stuff."

Edda finds that stuff exciting. She's told me lots about the stars and the universe; it's her hobby. Dad's also told me a lot about the stars. Stars are also Dad's hobby. But if you listened to Dad and Edda talking about the stars, you'd think they were talking about two different things. For Dad, the stars are physics; for Edda, they're a religion. That's why they were constantly getting in each other's faces. But Edda doesn't come to see us anymore; now Mischka comes and feeds us casseroles.

*　*　*

4:48 p.m. Kaiser Wilhelm is dead. The one who ate the baloney sandwich.

I just ran into Arnold in the yard. He was sitting behind the trash cans, his arms wrapped around his knees. "K-K-Kaiser W-W-Wilhelm is d-d-dead."

I was pretty scared and immediately asked what he died of, but Arnold would only say, "H-h-how do I know? M-m-maybe he was poisoned."

Poisoned. I didn't poison the dog. "Why do you think that?" I asked. Arnold punched the air with his fists. Arnold can do that fast as lightning. Way cool. Besides his computer work, Arnold does tae kwon do, which is evidently the only thing that helps with his stuttering.

"Kaiser Wilhelm wasn't sick, he wasn't old, and he didn't get hit by a car."

"Heatstroke?" I offered.

"Dogs don't get heatstroke."

"Why not? Dogs can get colds and cancer."

"That isn't especially helpful," said Arnold, and punched his fists in the air again.

"And now?" I asked.

"I'm going to bury Kaiser Wilhelm. And I'd be pleased if you'd stand by me in this sad matter, and together pay the Kaiser his final respects."

This evening we drove to the lake in Arnold's car. Kaiser Wilhelm lay in a cardboard box. At a sheltered spot, Arnold began digging like a lunatic. He was drenched with sweat after only five minutes. It was 8:17 p.m. by my watch. By that time the hole was already deep enough, but Arnold kept digging. I believe Arnold didn't want to stop because that would mean he'd have to say goodbye to Kaiser Wilhelm. I didn't want him to stop either. If Arnold kept digging, I thought to myself, eventually he'd come out somewhere on the other side of the world, in Australia. But Arnold set the spade aside, knelt down with the box in front of the grave, and then carefully laid the box down in the hole. "We don't have any roses," he said.

"Roses don't grow down here by the lake. Why don't we use some other flowers?" I proposed, and looked around for any plants with petals. But there were only bushes. "Let's use elderberries."

"They aren't ripe yet," objected Arnold.

"That doesn't matter. I mean, the important thing is that you've got to toss something in, right?"

"But not unripe elderberries."

"Why not? Maybe dogs like them."

I was able to persuade Arnold, and so we tossed elderberries into the grave. Arnold crossed himself and began murmuring, "Ashes to ashes, dust to dust . . . Can you think of a hymn?"

The closest thing to a hymn I could think of was "Lullaby and Good Night." I suggested it to Arnold before he could think of something even worse. Arnold immediately began singing, and I had to join in. "Lullaby and good night, flights of angels attend thee . . ." The great thing is that when Arnold sings, he never stutters. But, after the song was over, he began howling like a watchdog. "He'll never wake up again. N-n-never, ever."

Arnold finally shoveled the dirt back into the hole. And then it happened. He suddenly pinched a nerve and couldn't straighten up and began screaming bloody murder. He crumpled onto his side, all curled up, and began groaning loudly, "Shit, shit, shit."

Nonetheless, he kept saying there had to be a cross on the grave. Now, where was I going to get a cross? It was already growing dark, and Arnold's moaning was embarrassing me. Then something occurred to me. "It could be a gravestone, too." But Arnold was against that idea. "You never put a gravestone on a fresh grave, because the ground is still settling and the gravestone will tip over."

I was completely disgusted. He was getting all worked up about a stone! We had an entirely different problem—namely, how to get Arnold home. Down by the shore, I found a round stone and carried it back up to the grave site, along with a few more unripe elderberries, which I sprinkled around the grave. I found I couldn't be sad about Kaiser Wilhelm, because I was so annoyed with Arnold.

We had to leave Arnold's car down by the lake and walk home, and I had to prop him up the whole way. Now *my* back is killing me. "Tomorrow, I'll get the doctor" were Arnold's last words to me as I set him down on his bed. Evidently, pinched nerves help his stuttering too.

11:18 p.m. 23° Celsius. In America, they use Fahrenheit. To translate degree readings from Celsius to Fahrenheit, you need to use a formula, and this is it: Any Fahrenheit degree reading = 9/5 of the same reading in Celsius, plus 32. So 23 degrees Celsius is 73.4 degrees Fahrenheit.

Oh, great. I've now caught myself doing math during vacation of my own free will, and have learned that 23 degrees Celsius equals 73.4 degrees Fahrenheit. What I can't figure out is if that makes me a nerd or not. And that's really the question: What makes someone a nerd? Is it knowing that you can't bury dead dogs just any old place? Or that if you go ahead and do it anyway, you can't put a headstone on the grave because it'll topple? Or that pinched nerves hurt like hell?

I'm going to sleep.

I can't sleep. I read the letter again. "The red animal is dead." The red animal is Kaiser Wilhelm. Despite the heat, I'm cold.

THURSDAY, JULY 25

The streetcar woke me up with its stupid *Bimmmmm*. It's 6:32 a.m.! What good is summer vacation if I wake up the same time as I do during the school year?

I found two letters in our mailbox. One from Mom to Dad, and once again one from no one to no one. I leaned Dad's letter against a tin canister on the counter so that he'd see it immediately. But Dad hates letters. Especially the ones with little windows. Sometimes he simply throws those away unopened. Mom always used to scold him about it, to which Dad just responded, "If it's important, they'll write again." Mom's letter doesn't have a window, but the fact that she's writing at all is unusual enough. Usually she just calls or sends an e-mail.

And here's the letter from no one to no one:

> the animal is lurking
> you think that it is dead
> 5 animals will grow from it
> and from each of those, 5 more
> and so forth
> you think too much and yet too little
>)x(

If Kaiser Wilhelm hadn't died yesterday under such mysterious circumstances, I'd be laughing about the letter. I'm not laughing now. I've hidden both of the anonymous letters in my room. If the red animal does multiply, there will soon be 5 × 5 animals. And then 25 × 5 animals. That will then be 125. That's a lot.

I've made a mistake. Actually, there will be more, since you have to figure it differently: 1 + 5 + 25 + 125 = 156.

It's true, I think too much and too little. And now I've gone and done math again all on my own.

By nine o'clock this morning, Dad was already up and in a good mood. "Good morning, Victor," he said, not even annoyed that there wasn't any coffee ready. He said, "Did you know that your hydrogen atoms are fifteen billion years old? There's been hydrogen starting right from the Big Bang. Boy, it really makes you think."

A billion is a one followed by nine zeros. It looks like this: 1,000,000,000. Whew.

Dad really was in a good mood, because when he's in a good mood he always talks about things like this. He'll talk about red giants, white dwarves, core fusion, sunspots, and black holes. My hydrogen atoms are fifteen billion years old, and they sure aren't getting any younger. I've got to go swimming. Water to water.

I set my towel down in a different location today and scan the pool area. No red-haired girl, no turquoise one-piece bathing suit. It's funny, but when I think of that girl, I always think of Kaiser Wilhelm at the same time. Because of the red hair, I guess.

Today, I've got to jump!

Shit, shit, shit. She was there after all. I saw her at 10:45 a.m. on top of the 7.5-meter platform. She dove in without a splash.

That's another difference between girls and guys. When girls jump, they usually try to splash as little as possible. Guys splash a lot. There's one guy who can jump off the 10-meter platform and make a splash big enough that the people up on the platform get all wet. He has a special technique and always yells "Bombs away!" So that's what I call him; I've no idea what his real name is. He's the boss of the diving platform. Luckily, he usually only shows up in the late afternoons, when the 10-meter platform is open.

Bombs Away has a pair of neon-bright swim trunks that reach down to his knees. Once, another guy showed up wearing the exact same ones. Bombs Away told him he couldn't wear the same trunks; he pulled them down off the guy and held his lit cigarette against them. The trunks immediately burned up, or, rather, they melted, and they really stank. You don't mess with Bombs Away. But, luckily, Bombs Away wasn't here yet.

I went into the water and observed the diving tower from there. The red-haired girl was up there. I can't climb up with *her* there, I kept thinking. That witch. With her sympathetic witch voice saying, "That's how it was for me, too." Yeah, right. I mean, really!

I did at least fifteen laps in the pool, up and down, and was getting a stiff neck from always craning it to look up at the diving tower. To give my neck a rest, I swam another lap without stopping to look. And all of a sudden, she wasn't there. I scanned the entire pool. She was gone. There was no trace of her.

I could have jumped in peace. No witch; no buddies; no Bombs Away. So what did I do? I left. And now I'm sitting where we buried Kaiser Wilhelm yesterday evening. I'm thinking about the letters and the dark clouds of dust and wondering if dark clouds of dust are anything like a black hole. A black hole happens when a supernova dies. The collapsed star has such gravitational force that no light or matter can escape it. It swallows everything that gets close to it. It even said that in the letter: "They will swallow you up just like everyone here."

Who would write such a thing? And for what reason?

I didn't poison Kaiser Wilhelm. That bread wasn't at all moldy, and the baloney was only a little old. And if someone had put poison on it, then Dad or I could also have died.

It's dumb. Who would want to poison us?

2:57 p.m. Mischka was here. I should have known she was coming today. When she doesn't show up on Wednesdays, she comes on Thursdays. Wednesdays and Thursdays are her days off. She takes care of old people, and sometimes it shows. Wednesday afternoons with Mischka are sheer hell. Dad and I both think so, but we can't do a thing about it. Every Wednesday at noon, Mischka comes tripping up the stairs with a giant pot of food. It's usually some half-raw mess of vegetarian junk Mischka calls a casserole. A crocheted red and blue shawl is always wrapped around the casserole so that the food will stay hot. But it's almost always cold, so it doesn't make a difference. Although I'm pretty certain that Mischka cooks for us on purpose, she comes up with a different explanation for the food each Wednesday: "I had dinner guests last night," or "I just made a mistake measuring and cooked too much." She never has dinner guests, and even Dad couldn't make that much of a mistake measuring ingredients. What she really means is that she thinks we'll go hungry, or at least suffer from malnutrition, because we're a household of men. Aside from the food, she's offered to come and clean house as well. When it comes to our bad nutrition, maybe she's got a point, but when it comes to our housekeeping, she can take a hike. Dad's a real neatnik, and our apartment is never dirty. Nor is there stuff lying around. That's not saying much, however, because we don't have anything. We have hardly any furniture. Out of five rooms, we barely use two; the rest are empty. Mischka says, "You need a woman's touch."

Today, Mischka brought us chickpea casserole. The chickpeas were hard as gravel, and there was at least a kilo of garlic in it. Our dinner routine never varies. Mischka puts the wrapped-up casserole on the table, sits down, and is silent. We wait. We always wait. As long as it takes Dad to get there.

"You could wait a long time today," I told her. "I always wait a long time," Mischka said. She's right about that. Once she waited until 5 p.m. for Dad to get up. "But Dad isn't here," I explained. "He'll show up at some point, won't he?" she answered.

For a half hour, I sat there with her, amazed that I found it easy to wait. She shows up, we wait, we eat. Then she leaves. If only for once we could say, "Nah, Mischka, not today. We were just about to go out." Or even, "Mischka, if you want to know the truth, your veggie banquets are really beginning to get annoying." Or I could simply not open the door when she rings the bell. But no, I just accept my fate and do what Mischka wants. Even today, I could have gotten up from the table and said, "Well, see ya! I'm going swimming." But I didn't. I sat there and waited with her for Dad.

As a matter of fact, he showed up soon afterward. He clutched his head briefly as he stood there in the doorway. He'd probably not been counting on Mischka. Then, with a sigh, he sat down at his place. Mischka sprang up at once, freed the casserole from its shawl covering, and divvied up the grub. Even from a distance, the smell of garlic was irritating the lining of my nose. "Not so much for me," I said, but in short order I had a nice heap of garlic with chickpeas on my plate. When we'd all been served, Mischka resumed her place, bowed her head, and began to murmur. An amen punctuated the murmuring. And after the amen, she squeezed my hand. She doesn't dare do that with Dad, because Dad doesn't believe in God. I don't believe in God either, but Mischka believes I'm still capable of being saved. She looked at us both and said, "Jesus will wash your sins away!"

Dad bit his lip; he was on the verge of a laughing fit. He began eating and said with a full mouth, "You know, Mischka, I can live with the idea of God, although I think he's an invention of man, but what's this thing you have about Jesus?" The day was saved. When those two get into a religious discussion, I can always make a clean getaway.

4:32 p.m. Even though Dad quarrels with Mischka all the time, he still seems to be happy about her visits. That's good. Because Dad's sometimes alone too much.

Dad's just gotten back from the supermarket. He's filled up the refrigerator, and he bought a pineapple. We decorate the pineapple. The green stuff on top is the hair, and Dad ties a red ribbon around it. Then he cuts two holes for eyes, one for the nose, and a long one for the mouth. He sticks M & M's in the mouth. "What's her name?" I ask. "Mischka." Dad laughs. We scalp Mischka and cut her into pieces. The knife rips into the pineapple like a crosscut saw, and the juice runs out.

Dad is licking his fingers. "Well, have you written anything in that book?" I hate questions that begin with "well" and am about to lie. "I've seen you carrying it around," Dad continues. "You like it?" I just go "hmmm."

"You don't have to like it. You should write in it."

"Why?"

"So you don't wind up like me. *Have* you written anything in it?"

"Oh, well, you know. . . . Nothing important."

"But you *have* written something?"

"Yeah."

"Everything's important," Dad says.

I'm not so sure about that.

We cut up the last slice of pineapple. "Have you ever gotten an anonymous letter?" I ask Dad. Dad shakes his head. Then he looks at my wrist and says, "That watch is from your mother."

10:46 p.m. Still eighty-two degrees. It's humid and there's thunder rumbling in the distance. Maybe we'll get a thunderstorm. I just came back from seeing Arnold. He's able to move a little bit again. The doctor gave him a shot.

Arnold thanked me for helping him with the burial and for getting him home. He gave me a key chain with an alien on it. A small silver alien with slanted eyes. It makes me think of Edda. Edda was dead certain that there are aliens all over the place on Earth and that they are up to no good.

Edda. I haven't seen her in ages. I'm not sure she even still lives up on the third floor. Her apartment appears to be uninhabited. At first, there were four people living in it, but one by one they left over the course of the last year, until only Edda remained. And no one knows if she's still living there, because no one has seen her. Up until six months ago, she came by to see us a lot. Edda was great. She's got long black hair that hangs down to her butt. Very stylish. She always wore old black dresses I thought were pretty cool. I think Dad did, too. The two of them were always looking at each other. Maybe they were in love. I don't know for sure, because I've never asked Dad about it. And he's never told me.

Anyway, Edda came to visit almost every day, and waited in the kitchen with me until Dad got up. If he happened to be sleeping in late, Edda always asked me, "Victor, don't you think you should go look in on him?" And then I'd say, "Edda, it won't matter. If I go wake up Dad, all he'll do is grunt and turn over. Why don't you go—he definitely won't do that with you." But Edda didn't want to go check on him, because she was afraid that Dad could be lying there, dead. I thought that was pretty crazy. If you spend your whole day thinking things like that, you're not going to get much happiness out of life. But Edda didn't usually appear to be very happy, if you want to know the truth. Only when Dad was finally up and standing in the kitchen did two pink spots of color appear on Edda's pale cheeks.

The more Edda came to visit, the earlier Dad began getting up; sometimes he even made coffee cake for her, but he soon gave up on that because all Edda did was pick at the crumbs. Sometimes Dad gave Edda flowers. White lilies. For the most part, Edda just let the flowers lie there—like the coffee cake. So Dad also stopped buying her flowers. Most of the time they pored over star charts, and Dad told her of the newest discoveries, and Edda told him about the aliens. Naturally, those two viewpoints didn't mesh together too well, and the two of them began quarreling more and more often. Dad explains everything very scientifically, since he knows quite a lot about physics, but that didn't sit too well with Edda; she'd leave our kitchen with the words, "There's more to the universe than what can be charted or measured."

They really began fighting, though, when Edda started insisting that she was being abducted by aliens all the time. They'd show up at night and sit beside her bed for a while, watching her with their giant yellow eyes. Sometimes they would take her by the hand and lead her through the window right to their spaceship. But she couldn't remember anything after that. By morning, she'd be back in her own bed, but she'd be all tired and worn out. Dad didn't believe her. At first, he'd say, "Edda, you're dreaming it." Then he'd tease her. Finally, he didn't say anything, and in the end he just completely lost it.

I can still remember it exactly. That day, Edda sat down at the wrong place. At Mom's place, to be precise. That's forbidden, but of course Edda didn't know that. Mom's the only one who gets to sit at that place at the table when she's visiting. I still don't remember the reason why Edda sat down there and not in another seat. Dad noticed as soon as he came in, and he looked daggers at her, but he didn't say anything. Then they talked a bit, and I thought it was going to be all right, until Edda started in on the aliens. Dad hit the roof. He began yelling that he couldn't take that crap anymore. That she should go see a shrink.

"And on top of that, you're sitting in Christine's chair." That was it. Edda got up, wrapped herself in her black wool shawl, and said, "I'd never have expected that from you. Just you wait and see." She said that last sentence twice, and my blood ran cold.

Edda never came back, and I haven't seen her since. I couldn't even mention her name anymore, and Dad didn't have any interest in his stars for a long time afterward.

Now Mischka comes to visit us. Recently, on one of her Wednesday-afternoon visits, she said Edda had been possessed by the devil. Dad just said "Women!" and rolled his eyes.

Sometimes, Edda and Dad went stargazing. I tagged along a couple of times. To watch shooting stars, for instance. You can see the greatest number of them on August 11. That's the Perseid meteor shower. The Leonids fall in November.

FRIDAY, JULY 26

Asset-noc says
observe the heavens
the stars will enlighten you
)x(

Slowly but surely, I'm beginning to believe that these letters are meant for Dad. He's the star freak, not me. Maybe I should show them to him. One hundred and fifty-six animals and fifteen billion hydrogen atoms. All these numbers! And I can't stand math. If the letters are for Dad, they could be from Edda. Who or what is Asset-noc? It sounds like an Egyptian god or something.

I slept badly. There's another half-eaten baloney sandwich decaying on the kitchen counter, and there's an insert in the newspaper. The insert's about mattresses. All the different kinds. Support-foam mattresses with shoulder comfort zones and activated spring-suspension systems for perfect postural alignment. That would be good for Arnold's back. But that little beauty would cost you three hundred and ninety-nine euros. You could practically fly to America for the same amount. I don't even have money to go to the pool.

I'm saved! I mean, Mom also sent me some money along with the digital watch. She's never done that before. I just found the twenty-euro note tucked away in the envelope. Twenty euros! I can go swimming 13.3333333 times.

11:17 a.m. I've jumped off! I've jumped off! I've jumped off! I've jumped off! I've jumped off! From the 7.5-meter platform.

I walked to the swimming pool, to save money on the streetcar. Besides, I was in no special rush. That witch was standing at the entrance gate when I arrived. She said she'd been waiting for me.

"Why?"

"So you wouldn't get away from me."

"Why should I want to get away from you?"

"Because you don't want to jump off the diving board, but you've got to. Because you've made some crazy bet, something totally nasty. Like kissing the ugliest girl in your class, for instance." The witch got a fit of the giggles, and her red hair glinted evilly. I thought she was a pill. Evidently, I've been broadcasting my thoughts on some kind of giant billboard. Or Lukas had blabbed before he left. He'd be here at the swimming pool all day if he weren't vacationing in America. "Nah, I wouldn't make such a stupid bet. I've kissed lots of girls. They can't rattle me that way."

I really said that! I don't know what on earth I was thinking. Maybe the heat had gotten to my brain. The words just popped out of my mouth. Oh, man! Me, kiss a girl!

"Well, if you've kissed girls, then it should be easy to jump off the 7.5-meter platform." This witch was a real tough nut.

So I was stuck. I looked at the redheaded witch with her green seersucker dress and her white clogs, and I just turned into a remote-controlled robot. The witch began giving orders:

"We'll put our towels there."

"First some sun."

"Now into the water."

"First, ten laps in the pool."

"Off the three-meter."

"Off the five-meter."

"And now off the 7.5-meter."

Only then did she stop ordering me around. Because she disappeared. But let me not get ahead of myself here. The 3-meter and 5-meter platforms weren't a problem. At least not much of one. I was a remote-controlled robot, and I just did what she said: "Climb up, walk out, and jump. Don't think about it; don't stop and stand around."

On the 7.5-meter platform, though, I hesitated. About a quarter second before the plunge. The witch was directly behind me. When we were climbing up, her hands were all over my heels, or she was breathing down my neck. "Hey, what's the big idea?" the witch began shouting when I hesitated.

"I can't . . . not just yet."

"Nonsense," she said, and stepped closer and stretched out her cold wet hand. She laughed at me. Or because of me. Then she grabbed my hand, yelled "Now!" and jumped off.

With me. It all went very fast. The houses you see from up there zoomed past. I glanced down very briefly. A turquoise surface was rushing toward me. Just before we hit the water, the witch let go of my hand, and all of a sudden I was underwater.

It wasn't bad. Really it wasn't. We hauled ourselves out of the water and sat down on the edge of the pool.

"Well, how was it?"

I hate questions that begin with "well." "All right," I said.

"Tomorrow, you'll jump by yourself."

"Tomorrow?"

"Yeah. Tomorrow. You don't want to overdo it."

What a brilliant witch. She sounded like my grandmother, although I don't have one anymore. "Don't strain yourself. Tomorrow's another day. Everything at its proper time."

We let our feet dangle in the water.

"What's your name?"

"Guess!"

"Tell me what the first letter is."

"D."

Dagmar? Danielle? Daisy? Dorothy? Destiny? Dragana? Dulcinea? Desdemona? Daphne? Diana? Darcy? Those were the names beginning with "D" that came to me. None was right.

But the witch didn't want to come out with it.

"Oh, man, you've chosen such outrageous names, it ought to be easy to figure out mine," she said.

"Doris?"—"No."

"Dorit?"—"Ha ha."

"Dolly?"—"Ha ha ha."

"Don't laugh like that. It's dumb. What do you think *my* name is?" Now I'll turn the tables on her, I thought.

"First letter!"

"V."

"Victor. With a 'c' or a 'k'?"

That witch. And then I had a brainstorm. "Deborah."

"*Deb*-borah." She smirked.

"What kind of name is that?"

"It's Hebrew, I think."

"And why do you pronounce it like English?"

"My father's a Yank. But I've got to go now."

For some reason, "Deborah" didn't seem to fit the witch. So, I've decided to call her simply D. It's shorter, too. D stood up, shook her hair like a dog, and said so long. I wanted to ask her why she had to go, and about a thousand other things, but she just left.

Now, I'm lying here alone at the pool. Tomorrow, I'll go off the 7.5-meter platform once more. And off the 10-meter the day after tomorrow.

Sometimes unusual things do happen. I snuck a ride home on the streetcar because it's so hot and I was too lazy to walk. At the second stop, a woman sat down across from me. The woman looked like Edda. She had the same long black hair, and the same figure. Except she was wearing a white dress. Edda never wore a white dress. Edda wore only black when I saw her. The woman just kept staring out the window. Because I wasn't sure and the woman was also wearing sunglasses, I stared at her for over a minute. Just as I was about to say, "Edda, is that you?" she turned her face toward me, took off her glasses, and said, "You want to take a picture?"

She wasn't Edda. She had blue eyes. Edda has dark eyes.

Then she got up and staggered out at the next stop.

Dad was walking around in the kitchen butt naked. That's not unusual. But it doesn't happen all the time, either. Sometimes I look at his penis and wonder if mine is going to look the same way. I mean, I look a lot like Dad. The same eyes, the same hair, the same fingers. Yeah, my fingers. My hand is Dad's hand in miniature. So I guess my penis will look like his.

I'd just finished making coffee for Dad. He looked like a lost soul, with heavy bags under his eyes and a crease from the pillow across his face. His hair stood on end in all directions. "Your mother's coming to visit us."

"Mom."

When Dad talks about Mom, he always says "your mother." As if he has nothing to do with her.

"Tomorrow. She called early this morning. Why didn't you get the phone?"

"I wasn't here."

Dad actually doesn't answer the phone in the mornings, because he says that phone calls before eleven a.m. are about as dangerous as windowed envelopes. "Where were you, then?" he wanted to know.

"At the pool."

"Was it nice?"

"Hmmm."

"Want to tell me a bit more?"

"Hmmm."

"Victor. I wouldn't say 'hmmm' if you asked me something."

"Yeah, well, you were asleep."

"I'm tired, Victor. Driving the taxi takes it out of me."

"I know. But . . . you're never here, and when you are here you're asleep."

"Victor, you're old enough. You don't need me anymore." Dad sat down and drank his coffee. "At the end of the summer, I can take a little time off. Then we can go somewhere. Maybe to Italy."

* * *

I'm not at all sure that I'm going to like having Mom visit this time. She'll want to see my report card. It's not downright horrible; it's a C-minus average, but the note attached to it is lousy: "Victor must try to be less *phlegmatic*. Besides that, he doesn't participate in class." I looked up what phlegm is—it's mucus. I'm mucus, or my brain is mucus. That's an insult.

When Mom visits, I'm always happy to see her. Under normal circumstances, that is, and with no phlegm on my report card. But when she leaves, I'm often disappointed, because it's never the way I've imagined it will be. You'd think I'd learn, since it's the same way every time. The real problem is Mom *and* Dad. They don't fight or anything, but I know for sure that Mom throws it in Dad's face that he'll never be more than a taxi driver, and that he doesn't get up before the afternoon, and that I'm neglected. And Dad throws it in Mom's face that she left and pursued a career, spends more time traveling than she does with me, and that she's tight with her money despite earning as much as she does.

Of course no one says these things. What usually happens is that Mom sits down with us and has a cup of coffee, grimaces, and says that it's bitter. Of course she says that because she knows that the coffee is from the supermarket. She buys her coffee at Starbucks. Then Dad says, "You look all worn out." Which is like saying, "I may not be able to afford coffee from Starbucks, but at least I'm well rested." Then Mom says, "Victor, shall we go get something to eat?" Going out to eat with Mom means that I can have anything I want. Dessert, too. But as far as I'm concerned, if there's enough food for the three of us at home, I'd just as soon stay in.

When she's able to, Mom comes and visits us every two weeks. But she never *really* visits because she's always just passing through. She's stopping at our place between business trips to Hamburg and Munich. Dad and I just happen to be here. On the way.

I've just come in and flopped down in my room. And because I'm bored, I'm writing down the little things Mom has brought me from her trips. Since she left two years ago, she's brought me the following: A miniature cable car from San Francisco. A lantern—a red one—from Bangkok. A book about Vikings from Reykjavik. A pocketknife from Geneva. A matrooshka from St. Petersburg. A toy stuffed elk from Stockholm. An autograph of Bruce Willis from Hollywood. A silver dagger from Istanbul. A pair of leather slippers from Cairo. A didgeridoo from Sydney. A Krugerrand from Cape Town. A Norwegian sweater from Oslo. A sombrero from Mexico City. A pair of Nikes from Chicago. A Polaroid camera from Seoul.

To be honest, I haven't used any of Mom's presents even once. I really could have used the pair of Nikes, but they were too small for me. That's all the more reason why I'm surprised by the watch. It's the first useful present! I've got an idea. I'll photograph the whole useless lot of presents with the Polaroid camera.

Great. Dad just came in. Now he thinks I'm completely crackers. Because of the Norwegian sweater I put on for the photo, in combination with the sombrero and the much too large leather slippers. But he took my picture. Taking your own picture without an automatic self-timer is bloody complicated. The photo looks dorky. What I mean is that I look dorky; Dad looked me up and down. "All this junk is from your mother."

"Yeah, for the most part."

"She should bring you a garbage can next time she goes through Singapore. You can toss all this into it." He said that because in Singapore you have to pay a fine if you throw any trash on the street. Then Dad put on the sombrero and yelled, "¡Arriba! I'm the fastest mouse in Mexico!" Dad's actually the only guy I know who can get a tone out of the didgeridoo—even while he's breathing in. When I blow into that long, dark wooden tube, it just sounds miserable. I gave Dad the leather slippers, since his own are coming apart at the seams. They look good on him.

"When's Mom coming?" I asked Dad.

"Afternoon. Sometime between two and three o'clock," he said. Okay, that means around four at the earliest. Mom's always late. Although she drives an Audi A6 TDI. That stands for Turbo Diesel Injection.

I hunted for "Asset-noc" on the Internet. The search engine showed me the following: "Under your query—Asset-noc—there were no referent links found."

Something nasty's brewing outside. The sky has turned olive green, and a blast of wind has blown through the apartment. Dad yelled at me because I left the window onto the balcony open.

The handle of the window smashed against the thermometer, and it broke into a thousand pieces. There are blobs of mercury all over the floor, and Dad was cursing. "You trying to poison us?"

What the heavens poured down was pretty nifty. An hour-long spectacle: lightning, thunder, hail. It's cooled down a lot. I sat in the kitchen and watched through the window. After lightning, I always count the seconds until you hear the thunder. The storm was right over us. I like thunderstorms at night. Dad likes them too, but for a different reason: a thunderstorm at night means more taxi fares.

Then I went to bed. At 9:26 p.m. So early! But I couldn't fall asleep, so I looked at all the anonymous letters again. If you want to be technical about it, they all have a sender:)x(. That odd sign is surely a kind of signature. Close parentheses–x–open parentheses.

SATURDAY, JULY 27

Once again, there was a letter in the mailbox.

> asset-noc is speaking to you
> you fear the black 3
> watch the stars

for they know
)x(

Today it's cloudy. I skipped stones down by the lake. Not far from where Kaiser Wilhelm's buried, I sat down and let my thoughts wander.

Suddenly, a red cocker spaniel ran up to me, stopped briefly, barked, and snuffled. I almost had a heart attack. Kaiser Wilhelm! But the grave was just as we had left it. It's true the gravestone has settled and yesterday's rain washed away the elderberries. The cocker spaniel looked at me with his sad eyes as though he wanted to say something, but I don't know what. Now he's disappeared into the bushes.

Suddenly, everything's gone still. The air is heavy and I can barely breathe. I'm going home.

Between the lake and the apartment building, I stopped at a bench on Kennedy Square. I didn't want to go home. When the weather's nice and you can go swimming, everything's great, but when the weather's lousy, boredom's as big as the universe. I sat there thinking about nothing in particular, and especially why Kennedy Square is named Kennedy Square, and also about how long you'd have to sit there before you got a wrinkled butt. Kennedy Square is actually not especially nice. There's some grass and a fountain, and around the fountain, there are benches made out of metal. The metal is in the form of a lattice, and it gets sizzling hot when the sun shines. Like a barbecue grill. About the only people who sit on the benches are bums drinking beer. I'm certain the metal has already branded their butts.

Was Kennedy even ever here? I thought he only visited Berlin once. Besides, I'm sure that Dunant never visited every Dunant Street, and Fröbel never visited every Fröbelstreet. I looked up Dunant and Fröbel in the big encyclopedia. Henri Dunant was the founder of the Red Cross, and Friedrich Wilhelm August Fröbel invented kindergarten. I haven't the faintest idea what Kennedy invented—I think it was enough that he was President of the United States. The thirty-fifth. He was assassinated. It said in *Playboy* that Elvis assassinated Kennedy, that really Kennedy isn't dead and is living in some bunker, which you can find in the geographical location where the town of Bielefeld is supposed to be. Bielefeld, though, is an invention of the CIA and it really isn't there. Kennedy's alive and so is Elvis. Dad left the copy of *Playboy* lying around in the bathroom. He says reading *Playboy* makes it easier to take a dump.

I was just thinking about junk like that, and suddenly there was another cocker spaniel in front of me. "Kaiser Wilhelm!" I called.

"That's no Kaiser, that's a contessa," said a familiar voice behind me.

It was D. D had a stroller with her, and she explained to me that it wasn't called a stroller but a baby carriage. A mini-witch was sitting in the carriage. She had red hair, watery blue eyes, and five freckles, and was about two years old. Or that's what I'm guessing. I can't figure out little kids very well. She began screaming when she saw me.

"She's hungry."

"Is that your dog?" I asked.

"No, my sister."

"I meant the dog."

"Contessa?"

"Yes. What kind of name is that?"

"Contessa? That's a title. It means the same thing as countess." Dogs always seem to be much nobler than their owners.

"What are you doing here?" I asked.

"Well, you can see for yourself. I'm baby- and dog-sitting. What're you doing?"

"Just thinking."

"Oh." D whistled for Contessa, bent over her sister, and began going "coochie coochie coo."

"Hey, listen, do you think we can go to your house? I think Sheryl needs something to eat, and I've got nothing at home," said D, and I immediately thought of the granola that Dad always buys. Even when there's nothing else to eat, there's always granola.

So we went to my place, and while we were walking there, I kept wondering how D knew that I didn't live far from Kennedy Square. Contessa even seemed to know the way, because she ran ahead of us and stopped exactly in front of my building. Then she sniffed all around thoroughly.

Dad was still in bed, but this time I was glad. Sometimes he can ask the stupidest questions. D and I carried up the carriage with Sheryl still in it.

"I've got granola for Sheryl. Do you want something?"

"Coke."

I gave D a glass of supermarket-brand cola. "Don't you have real Coke?"

"Nah."

D got up and began rummaging around in the kitchen cupboards, as if she were thinking of moving in. "Contessa is thirsty too. I need a deep bowl."

Finally, everyone was taken care of and making slurping or smacking noises. "Cool," said D. "A television in the kitchen." Then she stretched and yawned. "Are you as bored as I am?" Then it occurred to me that I had rarely been bored in the past few days. I mean, not *really* bored. Not so bored that you'd turn on the tube in the morning out of sheer boredom and find everything on it boring, too. Or—what's even worse—that you'd begin to find everything on TV more interesting than your own life.

"Nah. Actually not," I said.

"Then I'm in the right place." Sheryl and Contessa were gobbling and slurping unbearably loudly.

"Do you know who Asset-noc is?" I asked, after the eating noises had subsided. D rummaged in the pocket of her backpack and found a ball; she tossed it to Contessa.

"Asset-noc? No."

"Do you believe in reincarnation?"

"No."

"In aliens?"

"No."

"Have you ever gotten anonymous letters?"

"No. What's with all the questions?"

"Come with me," I said. The kitchen's no place for

secrets. We went into my room, and I showed D my collection of letters. D laid the letters out side by side and looked at each one carefully. Then she asked for a magnifying glass and found the following:

1. The "e" on the typewriter isn't working right.

2. The letter paper is faintly yellow and not as thin as ordinary letter paper.

3. The envelopes the letters came in are lined.

4. The letters aren't postmarked. That means that someone is putting them in the mailbox themselves.

Then D had to go. Before she did, I showed her the whole apartment, and D was amazed that we lived in a five-room apartment but only used two of the rooms. "If I had an apartment like this, it'd look a lot different, let me tell you."

9:31 p.m. I'm already in bed. Mom was almost on time. My T-shirt was sticking to me all day long, because as soon as the sun came up, it got stinking hot. Mom had shorter hair. Up until now, she's usually had long hair that she put up on top of her head.

"Things just the same around here?" asked Mom, and looked around the kitchen. Dad shrugged. Mom seemed different. Often she's either harried or in high spirits; she talks about her business or gets upset about the TV in the kitchen. Today she just sat on her chair and, after the usual, somewhat strained cup of coffee, she asked, "Victor, shall we go get something to eat?" She looked briefly at my report card and laid it aside.

We walked to the Dragon. The Dragon's a good restaurant, but it's always full. We only got seats at the bar. I sat up on the bar stool and shifted around and didn't know what to say; I was still waiting for some comment about my report card. I started out by putting away a half liter of Coke, and then I almost wasn't hungry anymore. Despite that, I ordered another Coke and a tuna fish pizza. Real Coke, ice-cold and fizzy, isn't something you get every day. Mom only ordered a salad. Something with arugula and Parmesan. She never eats much since she wants to stay thin. Dad says she's too skinny.

We sat there on the bar stools and I kept having to burp because of the Coke. Maybe I'm not used to real Coke with bubbles anymore. You can't burp around Mom as loudly as you can around Dad, but at Dad's the cola never has bubbles.

"Are you and Dad going away somewhere this summer?" Mom wanted to know.

"Maybe. Later on."

Then the pizza arrived. Tuna fish pizza at the Dragon is great. Mom's salad hadn't arrived yet. Although I really wasn't hungry anymore, I stuffed myself with pizza, and only after a while did it occur to me that Mom's salad still hadn't arrived. But she didn't say anything about it. Usually, she says something if the food hasn't come after five minutes. Mom complains about everything in restaurants no matter what. If the pasta isn't al dente; if the wine is corky; if the salad greens are gritty; if the pizza crust is too thick. No kidding—about everything. And she always gets her way. Either she gets a new meal, or she gets a rain check, or she doesn't have to pay. But, as I was saying: Mom was different than usual. She just sat there waiting for her salad and not saying a word, and in the meantime she drank three glasses of red wine. And she'd come in her car. Usually she only drinks mineral water when she's driving. Everything was odd, but I kept shoveling the pizza into me as if I were on autopilot: bite off, chew, swallow; bite off, chew, swallow; bite off . . .

Suddenly, I thought of a topic I could talk about with Mom. Her silence was actually slowly beginning to give me the creeps. "Mom, have you ever gotten anonymous letters?"

Mom looked at me briefly, her brows knit together. "Yes. Why do you ask?"

"Who were they from?"

"Victor, you know, I think your teacher is right. Sometimes you really are *phlegmatic*—at least when it comes to thinking."

I was feeling out of sorts and so was Mom—for some reason I couldn't figure out. But, strangely enough, Mom didn't say anything more about the report card. Not even, "If this continues, I'll have to send you to Mrs. von Grützow for remedial work!" Mom and Dad have been threatening me with that for as long as I can remember. Why do they even bother, if my brain is just made out of mucus anyhow? But when it comes to my report card and Mrs. von Grützow, to my amazement, the two often seem to be one and the same.

Mom called over the headwaiter. "Tell me, have you forgotten all about me?" That wasn't typical at all. Mom's voice sounded almost harsh. Usually, she complains very gently and so sweetly that everyone does just what she wants. But today she said, "We've been sitting here a whole hour. My son has eaten his pizza; I have had three glasses of wine, and my salad still isn't here. Are you waiting for the arugula to grow?" The headwaiter mumbled something and my mother growled at him, "If the bill isn't on this table in one minute, we're leaving." She looked at her watch. The head-waiter didn't take Mom at her word. I did. After forty-five seconds, Mom said, "Come on, Victor, we're going. In seven seconds." She pulled on her jacket, and eight seconds later we were standing outside the restaurant. She grabbed me by the wrist, ran a few meters with me, and pulled me into the entryway of the building next door, since it was starting to rain. Then she leaned back against the wall. "Boy, what a day!"

"Saturday."

"Victor!"

The rain didn't stop, and Mom and I kept standing in the entryway. "The way things are going, I just don't know if everything's going to be okay," Mom said. I didn't know what she meant. No, that's not true. Of course I knew. I just didn't want to think about it.

"Are you and Dad getting along? Your dad doesn't look very happy. Is Dad happy?" She wanted to know if Dad was happy. "Are you happy, Victor?"

"Hmmm."

"How's your vacation?"

"Hmmm."

"And everything else?"

"Hmmm."

Mom stroked my head. She doesn't press me when I answer only with "hmmm." "Are *you* happy, Mom?"

"Hmmm."

Then it stopped raining and our "hmmm" conversation was over. We went home through the puddles. Mom's outfit was all spattered, and she wobbled a bit while walking. I don't know whether it was because of her shoes, the wine, or our talk.

At home, Mom got her stuff together and wanted to leave right away. Dad said, "You're tipsy."

"It was only a little glass of wine."

"One? But you had . . ." I broke off my sentence. I didn't want to rat on Mom.

"Can you drive?" Dad asked, and then said to me, "Victor, how much did Mom drink?"

"Don't know."

"Victor, you know," Dad said.

"Paul, it's my business."

"Christine. You're staying here. You can even stay overnight."

"You'd like that. No, no, I'm going."

"Mom, you'd better stay."

Mom made a compromise. She's a lawyer, after all. She lay down on Dad's bed for three hours. Dad had to go drive his taxi. It's been an eternity since Mom has stayed with us for so long. She even took a shower here. "You need a new showerhead," she said when she came out of the bathroom wearing Dad's robe.

Dad's up already. It's quieter than usual outside; even the streetcar makes less of a rumble. Sunday morning, in other words.

"What was up with Mom yesterday?" I asked Dad.

"Why do you ask me? *You* were the one who went out to eat with her."

"She didn't say anything, but she was different somehow."

"Different?"

"I mean, she drank three glasses of red wine."

"And what did she eat?"

"A salad. But even that didn't come."

"You mean she didn't eat *anything*?"

"No."

"So what do you want? Sounds normal to me."

"But she was almost crying."

"What?"

Dad stopped leafing through the Sunday paper, and scratched his head. You could hear him scratching; that's how loud it was. I changed the subject and told him about Kaiser Wilhelm's death. "Who?" asked Dad, completely confused. He was probably thinking I meant the real Kaiser Wilhelm. "Oh, Arnold from the fourth floor's dog? Well, I'll be. Do you know who Kaiser Wilhelm was?"

I said, "Sure. There was Kaiser Wilhelm the First and Kaiser Wilhelm the Second. The first reigned from 1871 to 1888 and the second from 1888 to 1918."

Dad looked at me, impressed. I only knew it because I had just looked it up in the encyclopedia. I surprised myself by remembering the dates. Then I blew it. I asked, "So, what's up with Edda?"

"I don't want to hear that name."

"I'm sorry. But do you think she's dead?"

"Where'd you get that idea?"

"Last week, Mischka was telling me that Edda was dead and that only her ghost was still in her apartment, and it would find no rest because Edda had sinned so much."

"Mischka. That peabrain. What she comes up with. She needs a man."

"Why?"

"It's not good to be alone so much, Victor. It all adds up over time."

Actually, I wanted to go swimming, and it's been nice out all day. But now it's clouding up and looking like rain. I've been tackling the anonymous letters. It's time I put some real thought into them. Here's the latest one, which I fished out of the mailbox this morning:

> the castle offers 5 times 5 doors
> find the right one

then speak the signs
)x(

Again with the fives! Which door am I supposed to find, huh? And which signs? So I counted the doors in our apartment, and if you count all the kitchen cabinets, we really do have twenty-five doors.

I'm a little afraid. Actually, if you want to know the truth, I'm really afraid. I'm only writing this down because this is my journal and hopefully no one will ever lay eyes on it. Here's the list of signs on our doors:

1. My door: a Simpsons sticker, "Be . . . Very . . . Afraid."
2. The door into the kitchen: a sign, "Weeds thrive!"
3. The refrigerator door: a postcard, "You're too fat for this summer!"
4. Dad's door: a beat-up sign, "Basta! It's good enough!"
5. The door to the bathroom: a sticker, "Kiss me!"
6. The door into the apartment (outside): our name-plate, "Forlands."

There's absolutely nothing on any of the other doors.

6:02 p.m. Dad drove off in his taxi.

Before that, I went with Dad to the flea market. We do that a lot on Sunday afternoons. Dad bought a new shower-head at the stall of a Polish guy, and a sofa at a Turk's. Really! A piece of furniture! I could hardly believe it. I'd never seen Dad buy a piece of furniture before.

He prowled around the sofa for an hour, sat down on it, lay down on it, and looked at the springs from under-neath. He found fault with everything and drove the seller completely crazy. Finally, Dad paid twenty-five euros, and the poor guy was glad to be rid of him. Dad knows how to bargain. He's so ruthless, I almost die of embarrassment when I'm with him.

The sofa is hideous. It's got neon red wool upholstery and giant gold-painted feet. But it's very comfortable and you can stretch all the way out on it. While we were driving home, the sofa stuck pretty far out of the trunk, and Dad kept saying, "Now would be a lousy time to run into the police." We carried the bulky thing up into the apartment together. I think lead plates must have been in the sofa springs. It weighed at least two tons. Then we had to try it in each room. Dad was never happy with where we put it. I said, "Let's just leave it in the living room. That's where it's supposed to be." Dad wavered, but that was the final decision. The living room (which is only called the living room because it once *was* the living room) has got a proper piece of furniture in it at last, and Dad said, "Now we can get the idiot box out of the kitchen." I didn't think that was such a hot idea, but fortunately Dad didn't pursue the topic. I lay down on the red sofa and found it truly comfortable. I was lying there just thinking about this and that, when I suddenly saw the star chart on the door. I'd actually forgotten a door! I mean the door between my room and the living room. The door isn't really a door, because you can't open it. At least not from my side. A bureau is in front of it. On the living room side, the door's been painted white and there's a giant star chart hanging on it. Naturally, I immediately thought of one of the letters: "Watch the stars, for they know." I looked at the star chart and tried to orient myself.

The star chart is composed of two blue circles. The first circle shows the stars of the Northern Hemisphere, and the second shows those of the Southern Hemisphere. The Northern Hemisphere circle would be the right one for us—after all, we're north of the equator.

"You looking for something?" All of a sudden Dad was standing behind me.

"Yes, Sirius."

"That you'll find down in the Southern Hemisphere. There, by Orion. We see it in winter."

"Why?"

"In summer it can be seen shortly before sunrise. But who gets up that early!"

Dad told me a bit more about Sirius. Sirius has a dark companion star, Sirius B, that is one of the densest stars in the universe—a white dwarf. It was first detected in 1862, and first photographed in 1970. "Sirius might have other stars," Dad said. "Sirius C and Sirius D. But they can't tell for sure."

I'm pretty certain now the letters are meant for Dad. From Edda. Only Edda could think of stuff like this. Besides, they were in love with each other once. At least I think so.

I couldn't get Sirius out of my mind; it seems to be a mysterious star, and I found out something really cool about it on the Internet: there's a tribe in Africa, the Dogon, that knows that Sirius B exists. They've known about it for hundreds of years. But how could they have known about it? It was only discovered in 1862! Sirius B, which the Dogon call *po tolo,* is just about as large as Earth but has as much mass as the sun and shines only dimly. It takes 50.1 years to orbit around Sirius just once, and the Dogon even know that. A scientist went and asked the Dogon how it was that they knew about the star next to Sirius. The Dogon showed the scientist cave drawings of dolphin-like creatures, along with a kind of flying saucer. The Dogon said that these creatures were the ones who had brought civilization to Earth. The Dogon live near Timbuktoo.

Sirius is only 8.6 light-years from Earth. Maybe people from Sirius did abduct Edda and everything she's been blathering about is true. It suddenly occurs to me now that the sofa cost twenty-five euros, and there was something in the letter about twenty-five doors. That's significant.

MONDAY, JULY 29

No letter yet.

There's something in today's newspaper about a landing pad for extraterrestrials in Canada. There are about three hundred and fifty UFO sightings a year in Canada. Every tenth Canadian has seen a UFO at least once, and there's an eighty-year-old woman who has been filming strange objects in the sky for twenty years.

Instead of a letter, we got a phone call. It was D. She said she was bored and wanted to come over. She said she absolutely had to let me in on something. I hesitated because of Dad. He'll grill me, of course, if he notices that I'm being visited by a girl. And then he'll explain to me that you have to use condoms when you have sex. Maybe he'll explain the whole gamut of sex from start to finish, although I'd rather he just leave the subject alone. At any rate, he'll ask me if I'm in love. That wouldn't bother him at all.

D didn't ask if it was all right with me. She simply said that she was coming by at noon.

When I woke Dad up at eleven, he said, "What, so late already? I've got to get out of here! I've got to be at work at noon today!" and he jumped out of bed with unusual energy. Despite that, he's sitting in his underwear at the kitchen table and reading the newspaper right now as if he hasn't a care in the world. I'm in my room on tenterhooks, hoping that Dad leaves before D arrives.

Now I can hear Dad padding along the corridor. He's dressed—I can see that through the door. It's 11:59 a.m. He disappears into the bathroom, runs the water, then flushes the toilet. The door opens; Dad adjusts his belt, and now he's approaching my room at an alarming pace. Quickly, hide this. . . .

12:05 p.m. Dad's gone. "I'll be back at midnight. Turn off the tube by nine o'clock." Dad always says that, but it doesn't worry me. I *televise* when I want to. He's almost never home in the evening.

* * *

11:51 p.m. I'm lying in bed.

D arrived a quarter of an hour late; I wonder why her tardiness made me so nervous. I was even trying to figure out whether or not I had time to run out to the store and buy some real Coke.

What a joke!

By the time she was at my door holding her baby sister in her arms, I had no idea what I should say to her by way of greeting, and so I asked, "Well, what's this thing you've absolutely got to tell me?" and so I, myself, began a question with "well."

"Not so fast, not so fast." D put down Sheryl, who immediately began to grab at my hand with her small, sticky fingers. "Sheryl's hungry again, and she's been jabbering about your granola for hours now."

Contessa had already slipped between my legs and was searching the apartment for enemies to bark at. Contessa really is a dreadful yapper. I told D that Kaiser Wilhelm, by comparison, had been a model of good behavior and friendliness.

"Well, it's usually the other way around—the male dogs are hyper and the females are gentle," D said, before I explained to her that Kaiser Wilhelm had been castrated and maybe that was why he was so mild-mannered. Then D looked at me all flustered; I didn't understand why. "Whaaaaaat? He was castrated?" She went all pale and whispered, "That can't be, that can't be."

"Why are you so upset? It's the normal thing to do," I said.

5 0

"Do you think it would be normal if someone cut off your balls?"

My ears turned bright red. I was smushing up granola with lukewarm milk; it felt like I had been doing it for centuries. When she saw the granola, Sheryl began grinning from ear to ear. I just hate granola. After everyone was taken care of, I asked D again, "So, what've you thought of?"

"First let me see the letters again." D looked at each of the letters with the magnifying glass for at least a minute apiece. I was itching to know what she was looking for! Maybe fingerprints.

"The letter sender knows you."

"Great. I've figured out that much. I've been thinking that something *really* exciting had occurred to you."

"The letter sender lives in this building." With the air of someone taking a secret oath, D whispered that sentence into my ear. Her breath was warm and a little sticky from the cola.

I began laughing, because D wasn't telling me anything new. I'd figured all that out already. I said, "You know, I've been asking myself if the letters are really meant for me in the first place."

D looked at me, astonished. "Who else?"

"For Dad."

D wrinkled her brow for a moment, then said, "But that doesn't change anything."

"How do you mean?"

"I mean about the letter sender living in this building."

I said, "As far as that goes, I'm thinking that this is a

woman letter writer. Maybe Dad has a secret admirer. From his taxi driving, maybe." D wound a lock of hair around her finger. She was pondering and I let her. I didn't tell her that it was clear to me that Edda had been writing those letters. "We've got to examine all the apartments in the building." I nodded. D really must be superbored to take such an interest in strange letters. Maybe her vacation has been every bit as slow as mine. Or maybe she's been watching too many crime shows. "Who lives here?" she asked, and I briefly filled her in on the tenants of the building.

We left Sheryl in my room playing with Mom's gifts. She especially likes the plush elk. I'd rather have brought her with us on our tour of the building, but D said Sheryl was used to being left alone. D wanted to begin with Arnold on the fourth floor. I tried to come up with a reason why I could knock on his door. That wasn't difficult—after all, Arnold had been wanting to give me a couple of lessons in tae kwon do. But Arnold wasn't home. I was secretly glad, but only briefly. Because then we went down to the third floor to Edda's, and D wanted to knock on her door. I said that wouldn't make much sense, but D rang the buzzer. We waited for a bit and then she pressed it again. Twice in a row and for a long time. Nothing. D wouldn't stop; she rang about five more times. Then she knocked on the door and we noticed it had been left open. D edged the door open with her foot and hollered into the apartment, "Edda! Are you there?" Of course, there was no reply. Someone who hadn't shown her face for six months would hardly reply to "Edda! Are you there?"

"Not here," D pronounced, and walked into the apartment. Her bloodhound before her, of course. The witch is totally idiotic! I've never walked into a stranger's apartment, much less into Edda's. Then it occurred to me that although Edda had been in our apartment a hundred thousand times, I'd never been to hers. Nor had Dad, as far as I knew.

Edda's apartment was empty. And by that, I don't mean that no one was home, but that there was nothing in it.

There wasn't even a sink in the kitchen. Under the faucet, there was a plastic basin, and instead of an oven there was a table with an electric kettle and a hot plate. Against one wall, full cans of ravioli were stacked; against another, carefully separated, were the empty cans. "If you eat too much ravioli, it gives you cancer," said D in the dusty stillness. "Shhh," I went. A naked lightbulb hung from the ceiling. D bent over one of the cooking pots and scratched her fingernail against the congealed remains of food. "Totally dried up."

In one room, which must have been Edda's bedroom, there was a mattress with balled-up bedclothes and a stuffed animal: a rumpled gray kitten missing one eye. D picked it up, sniffed it, and let it drop. "Eeeeeuuuuwww ... Gross."

"Then why did you smell it?" I asked. D shrugged. "You've got to investigate everything."

There was only a toilet bowl in the bathroom. The tiles were coming off the wall; the sink had been taken out and was leaning in a corner on the floor. We needed only a quick look.

The door to the last room groaned so horribly that Contessa began growling. This room was painted black. In the middle was a desk, and on the desk was an old black typewriter. "Wow!" yelled D.

There was a pile of paper on the floor, and D bent over to pick up a sheet. "Now I'll test the 'e.'" D inserted the sheet of paper, tapped a couple of times on the "e" key. Then she folded the sheet of paper and stuck it in her jeans.

"That we'll have to look at more closely." I had hit a couple of the typewriter keys—just a few letters, because I'd only ever seen an old typewriter like that in the movies. The keys were hard to press down—much harder than those on a computer keyboard. "Where's Edda hiding, anyway?" I wondered out loud. I had become convinced that Edda was still around and had lured us into a trap. The stink in the apartment was unbearable. It smelled of dirty toilet, scum, canned ravioli, garbage, and dust that had just been piling up.

Then we heard footsteps on the stairs. Contessa whimpered softly, and D pulled me and the animal behind the door. I hit my head on something hard. There was a loud crash. Something had fallen down in front of us. We looked on the floor and right into a terrible, scowling face. The terrible face was vaguely African—it was a mask. It was grinning nastily at us. The steps went by the apartment door. "We've got to get out of here," I whispered, and ran out. My legs had turned to putty, exactly like in dreams when you're trying to run away and you can't. D pulled the door to exactly as we had found it, and went calmly back down the stairs.

"Man, are *you* a sissy," D said once we were back in my room, where Sheryl greeted us with howls. "You really have the right sticker on your bedroom door. Be... Very... Afraid. Ha ha ha." I was glad to be back in my apartment. Of course it's a bit empty, and sometimes very lonely, but so bright and clean! Downright cozy compared to Edda's hellhole.

D cuddled Sheryl, who had been wearing my sombrero from Mexico and coloring in my book about Vikings from Reykjavik. Then D gave Sheryl a pacifier and set her down. After that she took out the sheet of paper with the typing samples and we compared the "e"s. "*Psssst*... look at that 'e.'" The "e" on Edda's typewriter wasn't perfectly aligned, like the "e" in the anonymous letters, but I wasn't completely sure. So in all seriousness, D proposed going back upstairs to test all the rest of the letters. "You're crazy." "No, Mr. Be-Very-Afraid. I'm just taking this seriously."

I was quite disturbed. Up till now, I'd been absolutely drop-dead certain that Edda had written the letters. But while we were typing, I had noticed that the keys on the typewriter were all dusty. Nobody had used that machine for a long time. "You're not as dumb as you look, Mr. Be-Very-Afraid," D said when I remarked on this.

D's just a horror. Now I'll probably be Mr. Be-Very-Afraid for the rest of my life. With any luck, she won't read the magnet on our refrigerator door and start telling me, "You're too fat for this summer!"

In the meantime, Sheryl had calmed down and looked like an angel as she sat on the floor tearing the book on

Vikings into shreds. In reality, she's a little devil. She had bit an ear off the stuffed elk from Stockholm.

"You know what Edda's apartment looked like?" D asked suddenly. "It looked as if no one had lived there for months." D was right. It had been that way. The others who had been living with Edda in the apartment had gone away months before; no one had seen Edda, and I hadn't heard footsteps. And that would also explain the stink. "We'll have to keep that apartment under observation. And we should go up to Arnold's place," D proposed. I was against that idea. D looked at the clock. It was almost 5 p.m. "I've got to go," she said. "We will find that letter writer, believe me." D put Contessa on a leash, picked up Sheryl, and said goodbye.

I'm not so sure I want to find the letter writer after all. What for? And what then? Go to the police? Edda's apartment worried me. It was unlocked and looked like it had been hit by a bomb. Where was she? It could be that apartment stank of corpses. I've no idea how corpses smell, but the smell was disgusting enough.

To calm myself down, I had to watch a little TV. *Romper Room* and stuff like that. It worked. Then I scraped the "Be . . . Very . . . Afraid" sticker off my bedroom door.

It's occurred to me that we've forgotten Mrs. von Grützow. But Mrs. von Grützow is a psychologist and educational counselor; she wouldn't be writing anonymous letters! Besides that, she's out of contention, because she's gone to the south of France for the whole summer. At least that's what Dad said.

* * *

Later, I went to the lake to stargaze. I borrowed Dad's revolving star charts, on which you can enter the month, date, and time of day, and then see displayed precisely the stars you should be able to find in the skies. But I couldn't see them. Maybe for two reasons: firstly, it was too bright. The city gives off too much light. I couldn't find anything except the Big Dipper and Cassiopeia. The other stars were scattered chaotically across the skies and made no sense.

Secondly, it was too dark. I couldn't make out anything on the star charts. It's true that the star charts glowed in the dark, but only for a brief moment. I switched on the flashlight to activate the fluorescence, but my eyes were so blinded by the flashlight that I couldn't see anything once I'd turned it off. Also, I didn't know which way I should hold the charts so that they would correspond to the skies.

Stargazing was annoying. And, after all, what did the stars know, anyway?

At home, I took a cold shower to refresh myself. Showering under the new showerhead is a joy. For years now, the water's been spraying to one side instead of straight down. Now the spray is once again full and even all around.

Dad was awake *before* me! He was wearing a Hawaiian shirt. "Is that new?" I asked.

"Yeah, it's the fashion," Dad explained, and I asked myself since when had Dad cared about fashion. He pulled a flyer for a department store out of the newspaper and said, "Look. Hawaiian shirts are 'in' again and I'm going to look like Thomas Magnum. My red Ferrari is parked outside." *Magnum PI* is Dad's favorite TV series.

"Really?" I asked, and almost half believed it. It's just a small step from a red sofa to a red Ferrari. "We need a new thermometer," I said, since I always want to know how warm or cold it is.

Dad pulled another flyer out of the newspaper. "They're offering digital thermometers for sale at the supermarket. 9.95 euros."

In the mailbox was the following letter:

> if you don't believe, you will fall into the
> depths
> you have seen the black 3
> and it will annihilate all

who remain in the house of sin
)x(

Now a clever thought occurs to me: the letters are from Mischka to Dad. She's got the Jesus bug and is always after us to believe in God. The letters could be a kind of disguised declaration of love. If you want to know the truth, I've always been afraid of something like this. Poor Mischka. Still, Dad goes easy on her; he's willing to discuss for hours whether Mary was a virgin or not. I'm going to show Dad the letters.

I don't show him the letters. Right now, Dad doesn't want to hear anything about either Mischka or Edda; I think he's thinking about Mom all the time. Sure—that's what he's doing. He bought a sofa and a new showerhead. And a Hawaiian shirt. He doesn't want to appear so unkempt. He's even getting up earlier than usual.

2:23 p.m. Eighty-six degrees. At the swimming pool, I immediately climbed up onto the 7.5-meter platform, and felt completely at home up there. Nothing to it, I thought, and just let myself fall in. In the middle of the jump, which lasted at least a minute, I suddenly started hearing a voice in my head that said: "If you don't believe, you will fall into the depths." The turquoise tiles seemed to freeze in the midst of Noah's flood; the bottom of the pool became the anteroom to hell, and I was sure it was going to open just before impact. A huge beast that looked like a red cocker spaniel would open its mouth and swallow me.

Well, the pool wasn't empty, and that's why I now have

beet-red arms, which I had extended to break my fall. Noah's flood is very hard.

Actually, I'd been hoping to see D at the swimming pool, but she's not here. I'm going home.

D was waiting outside in front of the exit. She was waiting there with the baby carriage and the dog. "I knew you were here. You've got to keep your arms by your sides when you jump."

"I already know that," I said. Contessa started sniffing around me, and I pushed her away.

"Hey, what are you doing? She likes you. She wants to make friends."

"Not me."

"What have you got against Contessa all of a sudden?"

"Nothing. Where were you?"

"Well, you can see, can't you? I've been saddled with Sheryl."

"I got another letter."

"It's about time we did something."

Big deal, I thought.

"We've got to scour the *entire* building."

I nodded halfheartedly and said, "We forgot someone."

"Who?"

"Mrs. von Grützow."

"Oh, the one with the moony eyes. She's not even here."

"How do you know Mrs. von Grützow?"

"Her name's downstairs on the doorbell directory. I've never met her." D quickly changed the subject, and we walked the whole way to my place with the dog and the baby carriage in tow. It struck me as kind of comical. We were almost like a family. D the mother, me the father, and Sheryl the child. Totally nuts. At first I walked behind D, but I finally found that foolish as well.

On the way, I managed to squeeze some info out of her. She told me the whole story about her American daddy. Actually, he's not a real Yank. He was born in Germany—in East Germany, as a matter of fact. But her grandpa was a real Yank, and D explained that he had had to flee America because he was a Communist. That's how he wound up in East Germany. "But Daddy says the truth of it is that Grandpa was in the American CIA and was sent to spy on the East Germans."

But that was just *one* theory. D went on to say that her grandpa had had something to do with the mystery surrounding the Kennedy assassination. That he'd somehow made a mistake and had been banned from the country. I don't know. Maybe he was just an informer. Or D is an informer. She followed up her story by asking me about Edda. "Edda once declared that she had been abducted by aliens," I said finally, since I had to tell D something.

"They talk about that on *The X-Files*; that's nothing special."

"You don't mean to tell me that you believe *The X-Files*?"

"Don't know. Maybe there's something to it. At any rate, I always watch it," D said.

I never watch that show, because it's all nonsense. Dad says it's completely unscientific.

"Has Edda got any unusual scars?"

"No, she's only got tattoos—a squiggle and a few funny marks on her arm and back."

"Funny marks?"

"Oh, I don't know."

"Maybe she only got those tattoos to cover up the scars?"

"And how did she come by these scars?"

"From being abducted, naturally." It was all crystal clear to D.

"That makes no sense. Why would being abducted leave someone with scars?"

"Aliens are always conducting experiments and poking things into bodies. That'll leave scars."

"You've got to be kidding!"

"And how do you explain the fact that she just disappeared? I'll bet the aliens have finally decided to eliminate her. And maybe the aliens are after others here too. Like you, for instance."

All of a sudden, it was completely still. No car, no person could be seen. A gust of wind blew a newspaper past us. It was brutally hot. Sheryl began crying, and Contessa began growling. I saw in a window a pale face surrounded by shining black hair. "There," I said, and pointed to the window, "there's Edda."

It really was. But only briefly. For no sooner had D turned her gaze toward the window than the face disappeared. Then a car drove past and everything was normal again.

At home we decided to make a list of the questions that needed answering. Luckily, Dad had already left. "You took down your sticker," D stated as she was going past my bedroom door. First we gave Contessa water and dry bread. Then we gave Sheryl a bowl of granola. Our list looked like this:

1. Who's writing the letters?
2. Why?
3. Who are the letters for?
4. What did Kaiser Wilhelm die of?
5. Where's Edda?

I thought of a few more, but the questions weren't part of the topic: 6. Who was D's grandpa, and where is her father? 7. Will I jump off the 10-meter platform? 8. Is Dad in love with Mom again? 9. And does Mom feel the same way about Dad?

Next thing, we needed to *examine* the building, as D kept insisting. Therefore, D, Sheryl, Contessa, and I went up to Arnold's. He was home. He ushered us into the kitchen, provided us with cookies and lemonade, and left us alone. He was doing his exercises. "He practices tae kwon do," I explained to D. "It's a Korean martial art, and it helps with his stuttering."

Half of Arnold's apartment was devoted to computers, the other half to tae kwon do. When Arnold isn't doing tae kwon do, he's writing programs for the Internet. From his training room we heard dull thuds and heavy gasps. A quarter of an hour later, Arnold came back into the kitchen, dripping wet. "I'll just grab a quick shower, and I'll be right with you." No stuttering. Ten minutes later Arnold was wearing a bathrobe, pouring himself a beer mug of water, and dissolving three vitamin tablets in it. "To what do I owe the honor of a visit by such great and noble company? And who are the two ladies?"

I introduced the whole group to Arnold and explained to him that D was interested in tae kwon do and would enjoy learning all about it. But Arnold wasn't listening and kept looking at Contessa. Perhaps the sight of her made him think of Kaiser Wilhelm. But he said nothing.

We had made the following plan. While Arnold was giving D an explanation of the best and most effective of all the martial arts, I would go into his computer room and look for a typewriter.

Once Arnold had disappeared with D, Sheryl, and Contessa into his training room, I took a look around the living room. Several screens were lined up on a long writing desk, and the room was filled with a uniform hum. It was very warm. In a wooden box lay hundreds of key chains with aliens on them. Then I heard a yell from the other room.

I ran into the training room. D was gesturing somewhat helplessly next to Arnold, who was lying on the ground; Sheryl was blubbering the tears that Arnold couldn't shed. "It's the nerve in his lumbar vertebrae," I explained to D, and helped Arnold get up. It didn't seem to be as bad as it had been the last time. "Dammit," swore Arnold. "It's all crappy right now."

"What is?" D asked.

"Well, everything. Kaiser Wilhelm's dead, my back is shot, and then there are those letters."

"Letters?" I asked.

Arnold's gotten two letters. I'm not happy about that. Understanding, of course, that anonymous letters are never likely to make you happy, those letters to Arnold upset my entire reasoning. My theory no longer hung together. Why would Mischka write both Dad *and* Arnold letters? Maybe she wanted to convert Arnold as well. So I asked Arnold, "Do you believe in God?"

"What?" He groaned. "Now it's questions? I can't move, and you want to know if I believe in God? You listen to me: even if there is a God, I won't believe in him, because he's a lousy jerk. Who would just sit there and allow me to suffer pain like this—" D interrupted Arnold. "May we see the letters?" As far as he was able to, Arnold shrugged, and said, "Of course. Letters that aren't to anyone are for everyone."

The letters were exactly like the ones I had gotten, only the message was different.

> you have lost the animal
> the black 3
> is full of evil intentions
>)x(
>
> conflict in channels
> channels lead to choices
> comes to catastrophe
>)x(

Arnold belched softly and then whispered, "This has got to do with Kaiser Wilhelm. He didn't just happen to die; he was poisoned." That's when I asked him, "Do you believe in aliens?" Arnold whispered once again, "Of course. Aliens are everywhere. We're all strangers in this world."

We asked Arnold if we could take the letters with us.

He seemed glad to be rid of them. He was lying on the sofa and inhaling noisily. "Breathing is good for pain. Proper breathing techniques can make a difference. Women who are giving birth can spare themselves a lot of pain by using proper breathing. All great fighters are great breathers."

"Just what exactly is this sport you do?" D asked. "I mean the tie can do."

"Tae kwon do? It's a Korean martial art."

"Can you break boards with it?"

"That's just a stupid trick. If you really want to have someone at your mercy, tae kwon do is the only way."

"And it helps with stuttering?"

D is really awful. The one thing that you should never, under any circumstances, mention to Arnold is his stuttering. I was steaming, but then I remembered that I'd been the one to tell D about Arnold's stuttering. Arnold didn't say anything. So I said to him, "Maybe Dad can drive you to the doctor."

Arnold kept quiet. He was offended. I said a hasty goodbye and hustled D, Sheryl, and Contessa out of Arnold's apartment. Outside, I said to D, "Did you have to say that?" and explained to her that Arnold was very sensitive about his stuttering. D said, "I couldn't have known that. He shouldn't be so sensitive; it's just a bit of stuttering." D blew the hair out of her face and busied herself looking at her wristwatch. "I've got to go."

Dad took Arnold to the doctor. He took him in his taxi right away because it was already six o'clock—time for his shift.

I wandered a bit aimlessly around the apartment, made myself a baloney sandwich, and sat down in front of the tube. There was an interesting program on that contradicted Dad's theory about our fish origins inside our mothers' wombs. No person is ever a fish inside their mother's womb. Or a dinosaur, bacterium, or giraffe, for that matter. A human's a human right from the start; that's determined by genes. When a human's still only two millimeters long, his brain is already functioning. When he's twice as big, he's already got all his organs—even the lungs. There's no evidence of gills.

In my room, a plastic bag was lying on my bed. Inside it was a set of binoculars, and to the binoculars was attached a note written in pencil: "Since you're already absconding with my star charts at night . . . Love, Dad."

The binoculars really kind of pleased me; I seldom get presents from Dad. And if I do, it's something like a journal. On my bed there was something else as well: Contessa's collar. D must have forgotten it. She feels that dogs should have as much freedom as possible, and that's why she takes off Contessa's collar as often as she can.

Then, with my binoculars, I sat on the balcony outside the kitchen and tried to see into other apartments. But the other apartments were all dark. You couldn't see a thing, and because I couldn't see a thing, I sat there anyway, thinking and peering in. D had spoken of the "moony eyes" of Mrs. von Grützow. How on earth did she know Mrs. von Grützow had moony eyes? She said she'd never seen her before. And then I began thinking about all the other anonymous letters. They seemed to make no sense, but I was sure that they were significant and that the sender was trying to tell us something. In Arnold's letter, it said, "You have lost the animal; the black 3 is full of evil intentions."

It's true Arnold lost an animal: Kaiser Wilhelm. But who is the black 3? The black 3 must have something to do with Arnold. The only thing that occurred to me about the color black was Edda. Edda. Yes, and she was living on the third floor. Edda is the black 3. But why does she have evil intentions? Did she have something to do with the death of Kaiser Wilhelm?

The other letter might have been commenting on Arnold's stuttering. But I didn't understand to what catastrophe he should be coming. "Conflict in channels, channels lead to choices, comes to catastrophe."

When it came to my letters, things were even more difficult. "If you don't believe, you will fall into the depths. You have seen the black 3, and it will annihilate all who remain in the house of sin." If the black 3 meant Edda here as well, then she wanted to annihilate all of us. But what is the house of sin? Is it our building? And why should Edda want to annihilate us?

WEDNESDAY, JULY 31

Dad left his baloney sandwich lying around again. He also left the butter out on the table, and there were two black flies gorging themselves silly on it. I shooed them away with a knife. The butter was almost liquefied, and I smeared it on my bread along with strawberry jam. Dad always buys strawberry jam; he'd get no complaints from me if he brought home another kind for once. But he labors under the delusion that strawberry jam is the cheapest there is. That's not true. Cherry and apricot jams cost exactly the same amount.

D showed me how to dive: backward somersault with a half twist; one and a half somersaults forward; jacknife; and swan. She told me she'd been in a diving club for a while. Her father had been one of the best high divers around—almost good enough to have gone to the Olympics. But only almost. D rolled her eyes, looking mysterious. "My mother wanted me to be a diver as well, and she put me in a diving club, but then I had that accident."

"What kind of accident?" I wanted to know, naturally, but D would only say, "I'll tell you about it another time. Now we're going to practice. That means you're going to practice."

Up until now, I've never dived, only watched it being done. D showed me a kind of headfirst dive that I could do from the three-meter platform. "All you need to do is let yourself fall forward; the rest will happen by itself," D said, and it was the truth. The dive was called the dead man's dive, and it's ranked least difficult. But you've got to begin somewhere, after all, D said, and added that I wasn't as un-talented as she had feared. All I lacked was courage.

Dad came into the kitchen at noon, still pretty sleepy as usual, and I said to him, "Today's Wednesday." Dad didn't respond. "Mischka's coming today." Dad groaned.

But Mischka didn't come. It got to be one o'clock, then one-fifteen, then one-thirty. When she makes an exception and doesn't come on a Wednesday, like last week, she leaves a note. But there was no note on the door. Something wasn't right.

"I'll go down and have a look-see," said Dad. He was ev-idently thinking what I was thinking. We went downstairs to the first floor together. Dad rang Mischka's doorbell twice. After a pause, he rang the doorbell again, but he was shaking his head while he was doing so. "She's not there." Dad waited at least another half a minute; then he turned around and we slowly climbed back up the stairs. I couldn't quite tell if he wasn't just a little bit disappointed. "But Mischka gets on your nerves, doesn't she?" I asked him.

"Sure, she gets on my nerves. But the others get on my nerves too, and she gets on my nerves differently than the others do."

"How do the others get on your nerves?"

"All they've got on their minds are their careers. And 'fun.' And fashion."

"Do I get on your nerves too?"

"Oh, you . . . you're just my Victor."

I wasn't quite sure what that meant, and besides, I was thinking about just who he thought the others were; the ones who had only their careers, fun, and fashion on their minds. Mom? All she's got on her mind is her career, and maybe a bit of fashion. But fun's nowhere in the picture for Mom. All she does is work.

Dad cooked us fried eggs. Eating fried eggs is a thousand times better than being poisoned by garlic. Still, Mischka's disappearance worried me. Far too many people have been disappearing in this building, if you ask me. Then Dad left. He had to take care of something before his shift started. What, he didn't say.

It's nighttime already, but I just have to write down what has been happening. I think the only people who live here are crazy people. But to keep it straight: I wandered around our apartment like a caged animal. If you walk around even a large apartment long enough, it begins to feel like a cage. I once saw a program about a tiger who had suddenly been set free after spending his entire life in a twenty-meter-square cage. He could no longer walk farther than three paces in one direction and three paces in the other direction. He died, therefore, because he was driven mad by too much space. But I haven't reached that point yet.

After a while, I went back down to Mischka's and rang

her doorbell a few more times. Nobody answered. Finally, I went outside the building and looked up at Mischka's windows. Although she's on the ground floor, the windows are pretty high up, because the building we live in is old and has high ceilings. All of the windows were closed, and I couldn't see anything interesting. So I went into the backyard.

Everything was quiet. Mischka's balcony door was ajar. I used the garbage cans to climb onto the roof of the garage, and from there onto Mischka's balcony, which sounds easier to do than it is, because you have to get over some barbed wire and then go hand over hand over the stinking basement stairwell. Giant rats who are nourished by giant creepy-crawlies live down there.

I was afraid I wouldn't be able to pull myself up, but I made it. I jumped from the railing and landed—on grass. All over the balcony floor there was grass growing, real grass, and there were plants everywhere. Tomatoes, beans, potatoes, and vines with real grapes, on stakes. But the balcony was only the warm-up for Mischka's plant mania.

Like all the other apartments in this building, you go directly into the kitchen from the balcony. There was a multitude of plants there, too. Mostly kitchen herbs, I think. On the range stood a giant pot; next to it lay a head of garlic. It seemed that our midday meal was still waiting to be cooked. It looked as though Mischka had left the apartment in a hurry. I opened the kitchen door that led into the hallway, and almost screamed when a damp *something* slapped me in the face. It was a leaf from a gigantic plant.

The plant had taken over the entire hallway and was crawling all over the walls and ceiling, over the windows, and around the corners of doors. I've never seen a plant like that in my life; the leaves were rubbery, almost black and as large as plates. No, larger. As large as automobile hubcaps. The air in the hallway was moist like in a greenhouse, and every few meters an ultraviolet lamp was turned on. Plants like them; Dad has one too, but only *one*. Mischka has at least twenty of them, and the hallway is just the beginning.

Mischka's apartment is as full and green as ours is white and empty. Instead of furniture, the apartment is peopled by every plant imaginable.

Each room has a different plant scheme. In one, cactuses are growing; in the next, rubber plants; there are orchids blooming in yet another. But the most startling room of all is the one with flesh-eating plants. They aren't as measly as the little sundews you can buy in the supermarket. The ones that wouldn't hurt a fly. No, these are horrid monsters with gigantic mouths that probably eat at least a rat apiece each day. It seemed to me that—despite the many plants—everything was very neat. There were no leaves lying on the ground and the floor was as clean as the floor in a chemistry lab. I began wondering whether the plants were even real.

Then I saw the papers lying on the ground. They were two of the anonymous letters. I read and memorized them.

> do not deliver the innocent to their deaths
> for death is not joking

and it will come to you too
if you do not
leave this place of sin
11
)x(

the black 3 is bad from birth
and beware of the sword
of the 4
leave leave leave
)x(

I set the letters back down exactly as I had found them, and was about to leave. But then I had the most idiotic idea in the world. I couldn't bring myself to leave the apartment without at least feeding one animal into the mouth of one of those plants! So I looked around for something edible. But there were no insects on any of the windowsills, and not one of the plants even had whiteflies, to say nothing of other parasites. I searched all the rooms. In the farthest room of the apartment, where Dad's bedroom would be in our apartment, I found a tank that had a covering made of glass, in which there was buzzing and whirring. In this tank, Mischka was raising the food for her flesh-eating plants—thick, fat flies, the like of which I had never seen before. I stood in front of the tank for a while wondering how I could get a fly out of it without letting all the other thousands escape into the air.

I'll keep it short. Because I was so clumsy, all the flies

flew out at once, and all that was left in the tank were the maggots. The whole room was suddenly full of fat black flying objects. Finally, I opened the window and shooed them all out. Another thought had occurred to me. When the last fly had flown out of the room, I closed the tank and left the apartment. I decided I was going to call D, but then it occurred to me that although she had my telephone number, I didn't have hers.

10:05 p.m. Mom has mailed me. Asking if I don't want to come. It would be much nicer in the country with her, and there are nice children right next door. Nice children. Mom still thinks I'm five and happy to play kickball, hide-and-seek, or cops and robbers all day long.

Instead, I'm here playing detective and have begun to understand at least part of the letters. Mischka has been warned too. "Do not deliver the innocent to their deaths." That surely means the flies that Mischka raises. The second letter recalls Edda again, who is bad from birth, and if 3 means the third floor, then 4 means the fourth floor. "And beware of the sword of 4." So Mischka should guard herself against Arnold! Although I now understand a bit, I don't understand a thing. I'm not a good detective.

THURSDAY, AUGUST 1

I slept until eleven, and outside it's hot as hell again. If you ask me, I think it's record-breaking heat, but I can't be sure, because we still don't have a new thermometer. I hear Dad in the bathroom. Quick, downstairs, before he gets the mail!

A blast of hot desert wind is blowing through the kitchen. Dad says, "Watch out; before you know it, it'll be autumn."

"But it's still summer."

"Yeah, sure ... but it'll happen in mid-August. One morning you'll wake up, there'll be dew on the grass, the leaves will darken, the air will be cooler than the previous day, and you'll know it: autumn's coming."

I tested the lawn behind the building. There was no dew. But it's not the middle of August.

Once again, there was a letter in the mailbox:

> how often has asset-noc spoken to you
> but you remain unbelieving
> do nothing
> and go not forth

you will regret it
11
)x(

Once again 11. Just like with Mischka. That damn Asset-noc. Where should I be going? If Asset-noc is out to get me, he'll be able to get to me anywhere. If he even exists. And if he doesn't, it's all just babbling by a madman. Or a madwoman. Maybe I really should go. What am I doing here anyway with a father who never does anything with me, and totally loony neighbors who are so crazy that any one of them could have written these letters? And D, that witch, who only shows up when it suits her.

D called me up and wanted to meet me at Kennedy Square. So we met, and now we've quarreled and broken up. This is what happened.

"You know, it's very simple," D said, after she'd purchased cola-flavored ices for herself and Sheryl at the stand and I had told her of my visit to Mischka's yesterday.

"What's simple?"

"There aren't a lot of people to choose from when it comes to the letters. Either aliens wrote them—"

"That's a joke; there are no aliens!"

"Who says so?"

"My dad, for one."

"Yeah, and how does he know?"

"Aliens are unscientific."

"Pooh. Nobody has been able to prove that they *don't* exist. On TV once, I saw people who had received messages from aliens. Those messages were composed almost exactly like your letters."

D stood up from the bench and spun herself around very fast on the lawn. Finally she fell down on the grass with her arms outstretched. Her red hair lay fanned out around her like a nimbus. She kept her eyes closed. I started to say something but she whispered, "Quiet!" It was very still in the small park. Suddenly, she sat up with a jerk. "Now, I've got it. Okay. Aliens from Sirius want to land on Earth and steal people. They've already got Edda and perhaps also Mischka. Someone has found out about this and wants to warn you."

"How do you know it's Sirius?" I asked. What did D already know about Sirius?

"All aliens come from Sirius," insisted D.

"Yeah? How do you know that?"

"From TV."

"And who wants to warn me?"

"Your father."

"But my dad doesn't believe in all that alien nonsense."

"Is that so? Maybe he's just pretending, and in reality he's part of a secret organization that's working with aliens to abduct people. It's funny, isn't it, that the letter writer is so well informed? The alien organization has plans for that building of yours. Maybe it's located on a universal communications site, and the next thing you know it'll be taken up into space. Isn't that in almost all the letters? That you should get out? And your father already knows. He's the one doing this, and he's acting as though he's just a harmless taxi driver."

"Dad *is* a harmless taxi driver!"

I was really pissed at D. Because she really *had* made me afraid, and especially because she had made up such stupid stories about Dad. She doesn't even know Dad. And anyway, I told her, alien abductions were just fantasies. Today, people believe in aliens just as they used to believe in witches, fairies, and elves. As far as I was concerned, Edda was either dead or had gone off to the country, but there was no way she had been abducted by aliens. Besides that, Dad also insisted that alien abductions were nonsense and only ignorant Americans believed in them.

And that's what I said to D, more or less. She was offended and left without saying a word. The stupid cow. I don't care. But there was something that did surprise me: how did she know Dad drove a taxi? I hadn't told her.

8:04 p.m. The best thing would be for me to just throw all the letters away. But then I'll never find out who they're from.

I've found out something fascinating on the Internet about the dog days. Long ago, the dog days were regarded as an unlucky time of the year. You weren't supposed to bathe in the open air then, because the water was believed to be poisonous. And if you wanted to keep your hair, you weren't to wash it in rainwater. Also, dogs were especially susceptible to rabies at that time of year.

My alien key chain lay beside me, the one Arnold had given me. When I examined the alien carefully, I saw a mark on its stomach—in the place where people have their navels:)x(. Maybe Arnold is behind all this. Who knows what he's up to with all those computers up there? Maybe he really is in contact with the universe. Except that he is getting letters too. Dad's not getting any. But it could also be that the letter writer is sending a few to himself as well, as red herrings. Still, I can't shake the feeling that Edda is behind this whole thing. Maybe she's been thoroughly brainwashed by some alien cult and wants everyone else to be too. Or she really has been abducted by aliens and the letters are cries for help.

FRIDAY, AUGUST 2

10:44 a.m. It's hot once again. We've absolutely got to get a new thermometer.

In the search engine on the Internet, I typed in "11." Almost every other entry was about September 11, 2001. That wasn't especially fascinating, except for the fact that the sum total of 09 11 2001 is 23, and the sum total of 23 is 5. My birthday is on the twenty-third, and Sirius goes behind the sun on the twenty-third. Edda lives on the third floor; I'm on the second. Edda's already crazy, and I'm on my way to joining her. Sirius is the dog star; it's the dog days; a dog has died; and D has the same kind of dog. Dad bought a sofa that cost twenty-five euros, which is also 5 × 5 euros. My hands have gotten so sweaty that I can't write anymore.

* * *

It was noon, and Dad was sitting at the kitchen table. He had been reading the paper. I said hello and sat down with him. "It can't go on like this," Dad said. Oh God, I thought, what now? If he starts nagging me over not making coffee anymore or that I'm spending too much money at the pool, I'm not saying another thing to him for the rest of the week. "What?" I asked. Dad didn't respond to that; he shoved the mail over to me. There were *no* anonymous letters in it. But there was a postcard. From Lukas, that dirty hound.

"Hi, Fictor, it's great here. I was in Roswell and saw a pair of real aliens. Oh, by the way—have you jumped yet? Ahoy, Lukas."

"Lukas was in Roswell," I told Dad. He rolled his eyes and said, "Yet another taken in by the alien hoax. I can't take that rubbish!" He shoved the newspaper away from him and said again, "It can't go on like this." He folded the newspaper and brushed back his hair. "I've got to make some changes. . . . I'm only forty-four. I can't be a taxi driver the rest of my life, or spend the rest of my life in bed just because your mother left me. Besides, this apartment is much too large for just the two of us. We should move out of here." Dad said that. Dad is forty-four. $4 \times 11 = 44$.

I've been sitting here in my room trying to figure Dad out. He's so sad; D hasn't a clue about Dad if she suspects that he's involved with aliens. She's just trying to rearrange the world to suit herself. I've literally known Dad since I can remember. No man is as unsecretive as he is. Mom is much more secretive!

I hear Dad walk by outside. He calls, "See ya later, Victor!" I don't know where he's going. "Where are you going?" I ask, and he looks into my bedroom. He's carrying a shirt and a small bag. He hasn't gone off like this for ages! "Oh, I've got something else to take care of," he says. Now, that's secretive.

The apartment is feeling too still. I have to get out of here. "You . . . do nothing and go not forth. You will regret it" was what the last letter said. But where should I go? The answering machine is on at Mom's. "Hi, Mom. It's Victor. I'll try again later," I say. D would certainly say that Dad's at a conspirators' meeting. Conspiratorial. That's what you call it when something is totally secret and part of a plot.

Once again, I'm pacing back and forth through the apartment like a caged animal—from the kitchen to my room and from my room to the living room. The red sofa is smirking nastily at me, just like the stupid star chart on the wall. I hate stars; I hate the universe.

Then I go into Dad's bedroom. I lie down in his bed. Everything feels the same. Dad sleeps on the right side of the bed, where the bedclothes are disturbed and it smells like him. This is what Dad smells like: a little bit like cigarettes, a little like sweat (because he's always saying that deodorant is unnecessary), and a little bit like dog food. I hadn't figured out the dog food part until just recently. I had always wondered just what Dad smelled like, and couldn't get it right, until one day Arnold opened a can of dog food right by me. It really doesn't sound very appealing to say that someone smells of cigarettes, sweat, and dog food, but with Dad it works, because he only smells like them a little bit.

The left side of Dad's bed is still made up neatly; the bedclothes are smooth and undisturbed. It's Mom's side, and if you sniff it very closely, you can catch a trace of Mom's scent. But that can't really be, since Mom left over two years ago and hasn't slept here since then, except for just recently for only a couple of hours. The first thing you notice about Mom's scent is her perfume, but under the perfume there is a very light odor of overripe fruit. That's one reason why I like to carry the slops bucket to the compost heap that the landlord made out in the backyard. It smells a lot like rotten fruit, and I think of Mom. Maybe I'm a pervert, because I find rotten fruit and dog food appealing. I've never told this to anyone. If I ever did tell anyone, maybe I'd wind up having to go see Mrs. von Grützow after all.

Mom could move back in here any time. Dad is still only using half of his closet; only two out of three towel racks are being used in the bathroom and, in the kitchen, neither Dad nor I ever sit down on Mom's chair. Neither Edda nor Mischka nor any other woman gets to sit down there either. Only Mom, when she's here. She doesn't know that, but then there's a lot she doesn't know.

A couple of years ago, I sometimes used to crawl into bed between Mom and Dad and scrunch myself down into the crack between their two mattresses. It was very tight, but I liked it.

I let my eyes wander around the room. On the opposite side of the bed, there's a huge bookcase Dad built that goes all the way up to the ceiling. You can only reach the top three shelves with a stepladder. The stepladder is always in the corner, folded up and ready for use. The bookcase is crammed full of books; they're even double stacked. I can't imagine that Dad has read all of them. But there are other things in the bookcase, too: a clay gorilla that's missing an arm; an old tape player; and a gigantic seashell in which Mom always maintained she could hear the sound of the ocean. Mom and Dad brought the shell home from a trip, and Dad said there was no way that it could be the sound of the ocean. Such a claim was unscientific. But you can hear a roaring in it; I've put my ear to it often. Mom left the seashell here since she thought seashells in a bookcase were tacky. Dad keeps the seashell dusted, and I've even seen him listening to it, but when he does that, he just shakes his head and says, "I could be hearing the pounding of my own heart."

What I'm trying to say is this: I know every last bit of Dad's bookshelf. So I'm surprised when I suddenly discover a typewriter. A black old thing—almost exactly like the one in Edda's apartment, actually. It's way up at the top of the bookcase, and I immediately jump up, open the stepladder, and take the machine down. A typewriter this old is damn heavy. Unlike Edda's typewriter, this one isn't dusty in the least, which doesn't surprise me at all because, aside from those baloney sandwiches, Dad is always very neat. I put the typewriter down on the bed and fetch a piece of paper from my room. I roll it in and type a few letters on it. Then I take the paper into my room, to compare it with the letters. The letters of the anonymous notes are much darker. The notes weren't written on this machine. Now someone's at the door.

*   *   *

4:55 p.m. What a crazy day! I'm going to Mom's. I can't take the loonies here anymore; anything is better than this madhouse.

It was Mischka at the door. She was white as a sheet, smelling of garlic, and begging me to let her in. Mischka! I'd completely forgotten her and her flies. "Victor, you've got to help me," she moaned, and went past me into the kitchen. There she let herself drop into a chair, and said, "You watch TV all the time. That's bad for your soul." I turned my head away from her—because the smell of garlic was disgusting—and thought, even twenty-four hours a day of TV is less harmful than one lunch with Mischka. But I didn't say that; I just turned off the TV like a good kid. "You shouldn't have any electronic equipment at all in the kitchen; the radiation is bad for food. But I've told your father that a hundred times, and he still won't listen to me." Then Mischka shut up, sighed loudly, and said, "Victor, someone's out to get me."

"Out to get you?" I asked as though I knew nothing.

"Oh, Victor, you can't imagine how bad the world is. Be glad you're still a child."

A child! How insulting! For adults, I'm always just whatever makes sense to them at the moment. If I've got to be left alone all day, I'm "old enough," but for other things I'm regarded as being too young.

Mischka handed me the letters I'd seen at her apartment yesterday. "I got these yesterday, and the day before yesterday!" She was looking at me wide-eyed with fear. I didn't let on that I already had six letters just like them lying around. "Besides that, someone was in my apartment

❈ 5

yesterday. He let loose all my flies." Like an idiot, I asked, "What kind of flies?" and so Mischka launched into the whole tale of her carnivorous plants and the fat flies. Then she sighed again and breathed the full force of her garlic breath into my face. "Of course, you don't know my apartment. You can live year in and year out in the same building, and still no one knows you."

Funnily enough, I didn't feel *that* guilty about having been in her apartment. All I could do was ask myself why she had to come crying to me about it. "Victor," Mischka wailed on, "what am I going to do?" I shrugged. In the meantime, Mischka had taken a loaf of whole wheat bread and a plastic container out of her bag. "Here," she said, "because I didn't come yesterday."

"Where were you, anyway? We were worried about you."

"You were worried?"

"Well, yeah. . . ." Mischka grabbed me and gave me a bear hug. The stink of garlic pretty near killed me. "There are so few people in the world who still have a heart."

I don't have a heart; I only have a nose. Mischka didn't just smell of garlic; Mischka also smelled sweaty. But anyway. "Okay, here's bread and garlic cottage cheese. They're both fresh from the farm. There's nothing harmful in them." Nothing except garlic, I'd have loved to say, but Mischka had already opened the container and was waving the cottage cheese under my nose. "You're such a good boy. . . ."

At that moment, the phone rang. It was Arnold. He was moaning, "Victor, you've got to help me." The nerve in Arnold's lumbar vertebrae had once more gone out of whack, and he had been helpless in his apartment since that morning. So Mischka and I went up to Arnold's. I rang the doorbell, but all you could hear inside were groans. I rang again, and the groans got louder. "Perhaps he can't open the door," offered Mischka. "And how are we supposed to open it?" I asked. Mischka didn't know either. "Kick open the door or force it, it doesn't matter to me; the main thing is to get me out of here," Arnold said from inside. So I backed up, gave the door a heavy kick, and there it was—open. I was pretty surprised and felt a little like Superman. The door, like all the doors in the building, had a pretty old lock. We found Arnold in his training room. It had taken him the whole morning to get to his cell phone.

Mischka immediately began taking care of Arnold, and was soon asking if he was hungry and if she should cook him something. Arnold only asked for a doctor. So I called the ambulance, and Mischka helped Arnold get prepared.

Then I left. Mischka stayed.

Later, Dad came home and I told him that I'd decided to go visit Mom. He was all sweaty, and he threw his bag on the kitchen table. It skidded onto the floor, but he didn't pick it up.

"So, now you're going to leave me all alone." Dad looked crushed. It had never occurred to me that it would matter to him if I went away. "You leave me here, all alone, the whole day," I said.

"But I'm here all morning, and I always come back."

"I'm going to come back too."

"Yeah? And what happens if you like it so much at your mom's that you don't come home?"

I didn't know what to say to that. Dad went on, "Ah, Victor, I had a lousy day."

He didn't want to tell me why. I hate that. Evidently, I was once again too young to hear something. I told him briefly about Mischka and Arnold, and that Mischka was taking care of Arnold.

"Then perhaps she's finally found a new victim," Dad said, sounding relieved. "When are you leaving tomorrow?"

"At ten-twenty-two a.m."

"Wake me before you go, so I can drive you to the train station."

I called D again this evening. But no one answered the phone. And I now have D's phone number as well as her full street address. So I guess I do have more in my head than just mucus.

D's last name is Zulinski. Deborah Zulinski. And she lives in Kimbernstrasse 11. The neighborhood is on the west side of town; I looked it up on the map. Kennedy Square is exactly halfway between our two apartments. In the dictionary I looked up what "Kimbern" means. The Kimberns were a German tribe that went with the Teutons to Italy to fight against the Romans. The Romans won. That was in 101 B.C. D lives at Number 11. Crappy numbers.

How did I get D's address? It occurred to me that D had left Contessa's collar at our apartment. On dog collars, you usually find a plastic tag that shows the address of the owner. I know this because of Kaiser Wilhelm. Of course, D had a tag like that on her dog's collar. That's it for today; good night.

SATURDAY, AUGUST 3

At the railroad station. 10:10 a.m., eighty-three degrees. The humidity is eighty percent. I've been thinking about this a lot. If the humidity were one hundred percent, you'd actually be underwater. But that's not so, because Dad once explained to me that the humidity index only indicates how much water *vapor* is in the air, and not how much actual water.

Oh, Dad. I just left a while ago, alone; Dad had wanted to drive me to the train station, but that would have been too stressful. Besides, Dad always dawdles so much in the morning, I'm always afraid I'll be late. So I just popped quickly into his bedroom and said, "I'm going now."

"You were going to wake me up," Dad said. He smelled of sleep.

"I'd rather take the streetcar."

"You're going to be just like your mother, high-tailing it without a word." Then Dad sat up in bed, fumbled with the book on his nightstand, and pulled out money. "Here's a hundred euros for you, for the trip." Now I'm sorry I didn't wake him up on time. He looked so unhappy.

* * *

11:02 a.m. The train left. I didn't get on board. I couldn't. I returned the ticket. It cost 23.60 euros. Then I walked through the train station and looked in all the stores. Not because I was very interested in them, but because I needed to kill time. On the departures board, there was a whole row of other trains. One for Prague, for instance. And one to Verona. Those were the two foreign-bound trains; the others were going to Hamburg, Berlin, and Dortmund. I've never been anywhere. Mom's been all over the place.

Then I went into the train station bookstore and looked at mangas. Lukas is really into them. You have to read them backward to get their full impact.

Finally, I began to feel a bit awkward standing there among all those busy people going to and fro and didn't know what to do anymore. It occurred to me that I should call Mom right away, or she'd be waiting around at the train station for nothing. I found a phone booth and called her office and told her I wasn't coming, because I had too much to do here. To which she said, "Victor, you're getting just like your father." She was pissed. But I was pissed too. Because I'm absolutely not going to be like Dad. And not like her, either. I'm Victor.

Now I'm here at Kimbernstrasse. There are apartment buildings, and between them hang clotheslines with lots of colored clothing flapping. The lawns between the buildings are brown. The first apartment building is pig pink; the second, piss yellow; the third, pale blue; and the fourth, a sickly green. D lives in the pale blue building. The buildings remind me of my grandma. She lived in buildings like this too. We always visited her on Sundays. She died over four years ago. She still hung her laundry on clotheslines, and I did pull-ups on the support posts.

I'm waiting for D behind the garbage cans. She'll come or go at some point. After all, Contessa has got to go out. Every day. More than once.

Nothing's happening. For as long as I've been sitting here and writing, nobody has entered or left the building. Does anyone even live here? The garbage cans stink to high heaven. Meanwhile, clouds have blown in. Heavy, dark clouds. It's even hotter and stiller than it was earlier.

Bombs Away, that guy from the swimming pool, has just walked by! He must live here. I don't know whether or not he recognized me. He looked at me as though I were from another planet. He was smoking a cigarette, and he disappeared into the building. The door clicked shut behind him. A gust of wind has blown an empty soda can in front of my feet.

After waiting for an eternity, I finally rang the buzzer by "Zulinski." Nobody buzzed me in. So I rang all twenty-four buzzers, and someone somewhere buzzed me in. I worked my way up the building and looked at the name-plates beside each door; on the third floor, I found the Zulinskis' apartment. I rang the doorbell. There were voices inside, but nobody came to the door. Ring once more, I thought, and leave your finger on the buzzer extra-long. "De-bo-rah!" I called, very loudly, and banged on the door. "Deborah! Open the door!" Once again, there were voices inside. "Deborah, open up!" Then I heard footsteps, and the door opened.

It wasn't D. It was a woman wearing sweatpants and a slobbered-on T-shirt. "Are you crazy? What do you want?"

"I want—"

"You'd better get outta here!" The woman had red hair. Like D. And the same eyes. "There's no Deborah living here."

"But . . . this is the Zulinskis', isn't it?" I was trying to see past her and into the apartment, but I couldn't make out anything. The hall was dark. It smelled sweetish in the apartment. "Contessa . . . th-the dog collar," I stammered.

"Get lost."

"But Deborah—"

"If you don't stop that Deborah stuff this minute, I'm calling the cops." I wasn't able to see any more. The woman had slammed the door in my face.

No sooner was I out of the building than it began raining. Raining is a slight understatement. It was pouring cats and dogs, and it made no sense to try to hurry. First, there was nothing to take shelter under, and second, within ten seconds I was drenched to the skin. And then, since I was soaked already and the streetcar didn't come, I kept walking. Wading. Streams had sprung up and were flowing down the gutters, and the water was ankle-deep on the streets. I could have been a contestant in a wet T-shirt competition.

I didn't understand it at all. Why was D's mother so peculiar? Why did she insist that D wasn't living there? I really didn't understand it. I understood absolutely nothing.

* * *

8:31 p.m. Whenever I look at the time now, I automatically do the sum total of the digits, and if it comes to eleven, I wait a bit before writing it down. 8 plus 3 plus 1 equals 12. The number 11 is scary to me now, because of the letters.

Dad's been on the phone with Mom. They're fighting. Because I didn't go. It's obviously a big deal, that much is clear. I can only hear some of what Dad is saying. "Of course I'm concerned. . . . But I can't just follow along behind him. . . . He wanted to go to the station by himself. He's thirteen. He should know his own mind. . . . I am not a stick-in-the-mud, and neither is he. . . . Victor's as normal as the day is long. He's not even in puberty yet. He is not neglected, and I'm not irresponsible. . . . Christine, that's complete nonsense. I'm not trying to keep him from you. Why should I? I have him all the time."

Dad slams the receiver down. After that, he stomps down the hall and slams his bedroom door behind him. Now it'll be impossible to speak with him for the next few days, and I'm to blame.

10:49 p.m. Sum total: 14. Numbers are driving me crazy. And now I've got this sum-total mania. It doesn't matter what numbers I encounter; I've got to add them up.

Evidently, the sums and their significance tired me out so much that I fell asleep. I've just been woken up by the doorbell, and I've been peeking through the crack in my door to find out who is ringing so late. Dad's got tonight off, and he's gone shuffling in his leather slippers to the front door. It's Arnold and Mischka. I can't make out what they're saying, but it must be pretty important; they're following Dad down the hall. A meeting of conspirators! They've gone into the kitchen. I've got to follow them.

What they *said*! The jerks! Now everything's really messed up. Mischka and Arnold were both pretty upset and were telling Dad about the letters. Naturally, Dad was surprised and kept saying, "Is that so? Is that so?"

"And it's been going on for more than a week. Letters, almost every day."

"And why are you coming to me?" Dad said.

"Well. W-w-we wanted to ask if y-y-you had also g-gotten any, and besides that . . ."

"I haven't been getting any letters," Dad grumbled. "At any rate, not like that."

I could see through the keyhole that he was bending over the letters. " 'The star is dying as did your dog and as you will, soon,' " Dad was reading aloud. "Oh, man, now she's completely flipped out."

"Who?" asked Mischka and Arnold as one.

"Edda. Who else? Who else in the world would come up with such idiocy?" Dad began laughing, but he wasn't laughing as though something were funny.

"Edda?" Mischka asked. "We went to her apartment. Just now. She's getting them too."

"Edda opened the door?"

"N-n-not directly. I've g-g-got a key. . . ."

"And we found letters in her hall. Six of them," Mischka said.

"Yeah, well, then, who could be writing the letters? Some kind of nutcase?"

"Not just some kind. He or she has got to be living in this building, or at least know us very well."

Dad began laughing strangely again. "And now you suspect me."

"You or your dear son."

"Victor?" Dad almost choked himself laughing. He was huffing and puffing, and it took some time before he had calmed down again. "Victor," he said again. "Victor couldn't come up with something like this."

Dad said it in such a way and manner that I was offended. To be suspected was bad enough, but it was much worse to hear Dad saying, "Victor couldn't come up with something like this." It sounded as though I were too dumb to be able to roll some paper into a typewriter and type a few letters. I wish I had had the guts to storm into the kitchen and insist that I had single-handedly typed all the letters, just to prove to Dad that I wasn't a complete idiot. Naturally Dad continued, "How did you come up with that idea?"

Mischka was sighing. "The poor kid. He's alone so much of the time, and no one's paying attention to him. Now he's begun hanging out in the neighborhood with this strange girl. I've no idea where he met her. As I said, I worry about Victor. The child is alone too much. And he's so bored that he evidently climbed into my apartment and set all my flies loose," said Mischka, and then started explaining to Dad why she needed a whole cage of flies. "Read it for yourself. You see, it says: 'Do not deliver the innocent to their deaths for death is not joking and it will come to you too if you do not leave this place of sin.' By the innocent, he means the flies."

"Victor has always loved animals."

"But it seems that he doesn't love people very much."

"Hmmm . . . How do you know that Victor was in your apartment?"

"I saw h-h-him."

"That aside, I still feel that your evidence is somewhat weak. What do the letters have to do with your apartment? It seems to me that I'd have more reason to compose these letters."

"Yes, you would."

Dad laughed bitterly. "I'm really not interested in that kind of idiocy."

"We didn't think so. But who else is there, then?"

"Grützow."

"But she's in the south of France."

"Then she's probably writing them from there."

"The letters haven't been stamped."

"I'll ask Victor myself. In the morning."

That was Dad.

They went on talking and talking and talking. I came back to bed, and now I can't fall asleep. What if the letters really were written by me? It could have happened this way: I was abducted by aliens who forced me to write the letters. Naturally, I couldn't remember anything, because the aliens altered my memory. I read that there are very specific signs you can use to recognize whether someone has been abducted by aliens. Those signs include disturbed sleep with nightmares; nosebleeds; scars of unknown origin; and fear of being alone. I frequently have nosebleeds and bad dreams. I have scars of unknown origin, and I don't like being alone.

Things are getting too hot to handle here. Tomorrow is going to be a day full of hassles. Mom is pissed, Dad is pissed, and Mischka and Arnold are suspicious of me. I think I'm going to beat it before any of those sleepyheads wake up. I'm setting the alarm clock for five-thirty.

SUNDAY, AUGUST 4

5:33 a.m. Sum total: 11. Stay in bed for one more minute. 5:52 a.m. Sum total: 12. One minute turned into nineteen. I'm dog tired and wondering whether running away won't make everyone more suspicious of me. But my mind's made up. I'm leaving, and it'll be some time before I come back here.

7:04 a.m. Sum total: 11. Kennedy Square. Sunday mornings are really dead as a doornail. There have only been a couple of people out taking their dogs for a walk. It is too early. I could have gotten up two hours later, and then I wouldn't be so tired. And Dad wouldn't have noticed anyway. It'll definitely be really hot today. I saw a thermometer on the way over here that was already registering seventy-eight degrees.

Since I was so tired, I lay down on the lawn. Fall must still be far away, because there was no dew on the grass. I dozed for a bit. There's still no one up and about.

It's getting warmer and warmer. Only now do I see that there are signs posted all over Kennedy Square:

> RED COCKER SPANIEL MISSING
> PLEASE, *PLEASE* CALL IF YOU HAVE SEEN OR
> FOUND MY DOG!!
> SHE IS TWO YEARS OLD, ANSWERS TO THE
> NAME CONTESSA,
> AND VANISHED WITHOUT A TRACE HERE AT
> KENNEDY SQUARE ON AUGUST 3RD, AROUND
> 9 IN THE MORNING.
> TELEPHONE: 0179-11 26 114
> REWARD FOR FINDER!

What? Contessa has run away? Maybe that's the reason D hasn't called. She loves that dog so much. It's now 10:02 a.m. Sum total: 3.

I ripped down one of the signs and took it into a telephone booth. The number was different from the one I found on the collar, but D also has a cell phone! It occurred to me that there were a lot of elevens in it. The sum total of the telephone number is thirty-three and thirty-three divided by three equals . . .

Despite still being sleepy, I had an idea and dialed the

number. A woman with an unfriendly voice answered. In a fake accent, I said, "Heinemann here; I'm calling about the dog."

"Oh yeah, like I need another joker . . ." At which point you could hear in the background, "Mom, don't hang up, maybe this time it's for real." Shortly thereafter, I could hear someone breathing heavily into my ear. "Hello, do you have my dog?" It was D.

I cleared my throat, and said in my deepest voice, "I've seen your dog."

"When?"

"This morning."

"Where?"

"At the lake. I'd be happy to meet you."

"Listen to me," D said. "Five people have already called here. Two of the guys wanted to meet me, one of them said he'd just eaten my dog in a Chinese restaurant, and there were two grannies who had confused cocker spaniels with dachshunds. You're going to have to tell me something about my dog."

I hadn't counted on that, but I know Contessa. "When you call 'Contessa,' she raises her head and cocks her left ear."

"Go on."

"She's got a kink in her tail."

"Hmmmm . . . was she alone?"

"No. A black-haired lady had her on a leash." That was made up, of course.

"I see. And where did they go?"

"That's kind of hard to explain. That's why I'd like to meet you."

"Why can't you explain it to me now?"

"Because it's too complicated."

D said nothing for a bit. Then, "Okay, I'm coming. You'll recognize me by my hair. It's the same color as my dog's."

5:58 p.m. Sum total: 18. Home again. Actually, I really just wanted to get lost, but I've changed my mind. I'm groggy and achingly grateful that Dad's off at work. He's left me a note. "Victor, call the taxi dispatcher when you come home. Dad."

But, to begin at the beginning: After about a quarter of an hour, D showed up at the lake. She was alone and had put her hair up on top of her head in a kind of ponytail. She was wearing a loose pink top and a pair of shiny red track pants. There were spots on the pants, and D was red in the face. She looked different.

"Victor?"

"Hello, Deborah."

She didn't answer and wanted to keep going. Then she stopped and said, "Victor, I wish you'd go. I'm waiting here for someone."

"Here I am," I said.

D isn't stupid. She caught on immediately, and she practically jumped down my throat. "Victor, you pig! This beats everything!" I wasn't prepared for that, but she was already running away. "Deborah," I yelled, and ran after her, and finally nabbed her by the back of her pants.

"Leave off! I don't want to have anything more to do with you!" she screeched.

"Deborah, I just wanted to . . ."

"What did you just want?"

I explained to her that I'd been trying to reach her for days, and that I hadn't meant to upset her.

"Is that your explanation?"

"Yes."

"And how did you know my address?"

"It was on the tag on the dog collar. You left it at my place."

"It's been with you? No one will believe the dog is mine without any identification. So it's no good calling the dog pound. Did you bring the collar with you?"

"No."

"Get it!"

"Now?"

"Yes, right now."

"First you've got to accept my apology."

"And if I don't accept it?"

"Then you won't get the collar back."

D shut up for a minute, and then she asked, "Why did you come knocking at my door?"

"Is that against the law?"

"My family is none of your business."

"Oh, but it's okay for you to come over to my place? My family is none of your business either."

"But I *can* come see you. That's the difference."

I had no idea why that made a difference. "Your mother is a bit odd."

"Yeah? Yours is odd too."

"You don't even know her."

"You don't know mine, either."

I sighed, because it all made no sense. "I'm sorry. I didn't know that your mother doesn't like visitors."

"You don't know that at all."

Suddenly D began weeping. Just like that. Well, not just like that. I'm guessing it was because of Contessa. I took her hand and we walked back to my building together.

There, I gave D the collar, and she stroked it as if she had found Contessa.

"Can I use your phone?" asked D. "Our phone is fluky, and there's only a few euros left on my cell phone."

"Sure."

I brought the phone into the kitchen, and she called all the pounds in the city and all the animal hospitals. There were only answering machines on at the veterinarians'. "Shitty Sunday. Who invented this miserable day?" she said, cursing. She stared at her list of phone numbers and kennel addresses. It was already all crumpled. She seemed to shrink as she sat there, until finally she was all curled up on her seat.

"Are you hungry?" I asked her. She nodded. I warmed up some Vienna sausages. She put about a pound of ketchup on each bite, and it spattered all over her shirt. "Shitty ketchup," she cursed, and dabbed halfheartedly at her T-shirt with a wet dishrag until it was one whole dark stain. A couple of tears rolled down her cheeks and she said, "Shitty T-shirt."

I offered her a T-shirt of my own, but she waved it away. "Do you want some chocolate pudding?" I asked, but she didn't answer me, because she had fallen asleep at the kitchen table.

She slept for over an hour. I didn't want to wake her up.

8:41 p.m. Sum total: 13. I should have woken her up. "What time is it?" D asked when she woke up.

"Almost nine."

"Why didn't you wake me up?" she shrieked.

"You were sleeping so peacefully."

"You're not to watch me when I'm sleeping. You ... jackass." Then she ran around the kitchen madly looking for her stuff.

"Do you have to go home?" I asked.

"Stupid question. What do you think?"

"It's not such a big deal if you're a little late."

"You don't know my mother."

"I do."

"You don't know her."

I had the sense to keep quiet; the subject was obviously a touchy one.

MONDAY, AUGUST 5

I've been awake for an hour. Dad came storming in earlier and was really annoyed when he saw me sleeping. At first I didn't understand why he was so upset, but little by little, things came into focus.

Dad was pissed as hell because I had forgotten to call the taxi dispatcher yesterday to say that I had made it home in one piece. What was I thinking, to simply run away without a word? Did I have any idea what he had gone through last night? "If you don't like it here, then you can go to your mother's!" he growled, and of course he also wanted to know what was up with the letters and just who I was hanging out with. He got louder and louder; so loud that the windows rattled. The louder he got, the less and less I felt like saying anything. But that only made him madder. "Answer me," he yelled, but I kept quiet. "Don't sit on that bed as if you wouldn't harm a fly. . . . And on the subject of flies, just what did you think you had lost in Mischka's apartment? That beats all!"

Dad stood right over me, and I could smell the sweaty odor of the taxi on him. I couldn't speak, and I didn't want to. For weeks now, it hasn't mattered to him what I was doing or what was up with me. I kept quiet, but that was a mistake, because suddenly Dad grabbed me and shook me. "Talk to me, Victor." And because I still didn't say anything, he slapped me. Right in the face. That startled him so much, all he could do was stare at me, and shortly afterward, he ran from the room.

My cheek is bright red. Dad has never hit me before. I'll never speak to him again.

Dad shuffled around the apartment for a bit. I heard the door to the bathroom, then the kitchen door, then nothing for a while; then the kitchen door again, and finally the door to his bedroom. At last the coast was clear. In the kitchen lay a baloney sandwich; the butter had been left out on the kitchen table. It was slowly melting. I left everything there and shook the can of ground coffee into the trash. I did the same with the granola, Dad's elixir of life. Dad can just see how he makes out without coffee and granola! Then the telephone rang. It was D. In a weak voice, she said, "Victor, you've got to help me."

"What's the matter?"

"Contessa. I don't think she'll ever come back. I'm so depressed."

I hemmed and hawed a bit, and D was sniffling on the other end of the line. Then I said, "You'll find her for sure; a dog can't just simply vanish."

"But she's not wearing her ID."

"You'll find her."

"Victor!"

I had no idea how I was supposed to help her. Let alone how I should comfort her. Only terrible things had been happening to me, too. Should I say that a dognapper had gotten Contessa and sold her to a lab? Or that aliens had abducted her, in order to mutate her into a super-intelligent giant cocker spaniel to take over the earth? That would just be crap.

At any rate, it wouldn't bring D any peace. "Can we meet?" D wanted to know.

"Swimming pool?" I blurted.

"Nah, that won't work."

"Why not?"

"It just won't. Kennedy Square is better. Maybe there'll be people there we can ask about Contessa. I've already done that, but maybe a bit more will help."

I'm sitting on the griddle benches at Kennedy Square and getting myself a grilled butt. Someone's eating donuts next to me, and I'm getting hungry. D hasn't arrived yet. I've been waiting for a whole half hour. I'm writing out of bore-dom. The guy sitting next to me keeps sneaking peeks at my journal. Actually, I wanted to throw it away because of my anger at Dad, but then I decided it would be a shame. I've al-ready written down so much in it, and—if you really think about it—it's almost a mystery story. Who is the perpetra-tor? If this were a film script, what would be the most excit-ing solution? Don't know. But I know what the final scene would be. The hero would dive from the ten-meter platform. With everyone watching. And when he climbed out of the pool, the girl of his dreams would be waiting and they'd kiss.

The guy next to me just keeps staring and staring. Has he never seen someone writing?

"That gonna be *Buddenbrooks*?" the guy finally asks.

"Who's Buddenbrooks?"

"Beats me." The guy has his mouth full and begins laughing. "Ha ha ha, a kid who writes in a diary."

I look at the guy. "I'll bet you can't write at all. You can't even eat." Half of the donut has landed on his pants. Today isn't a good day. Now I'm sitting on the grass after buying myself a donut. Delicious. I still have the hundred euros from Dad. He's not going to get it back.

It's amazing how many creatures have disappeared recently. Edda's gone; Kaiser Wilhelm vanished in an especially final way; Contessa is lost; and if D doesn't show up soon, I'll just have to add her to the list. But someone's also resurfaced, and that's Mrs. von Grützow. I just saw her in front of the building as I was on my way over here. She was standing in the entryway with two boxes, her arm in a splint and supported by a sling around her neck. "Hello, Fictor," she greeted me. "Fictor, your timing is just perfect. Could you please help me?" A lot of people have asked me for help recently. But Grützow is the first who has said please. "I thought you were on vacation," I answered, but Grützow just pointed to her arm. "Car accident. Concussion, whiplash, and a broken arm. And after only fifty kilometers. Great. They just let me out of the hospital the day before yesterday."

In one of the boxes was a computer with accessories; I carried it in for her. It was only a couple of stairs. It was the first time I'd been in her office. "Do you understand computers, Fictor?" she asked me.

"A bit."

"Very well, Fictor, then maybe you could help me. Just take it out of the box, hook the cable up, and plug the system in?"

"I can do that," I said, "but not just now, and only if you'll no longer call me Fictor."

Grützow turned beet red. "Oh, Fictor, I am sorry. I'll pay more attention. . . . But couldn't you at least unpack the box? Now? And then we'll make an appointment."

An appointment with Grützow! Pretty soon, she'll want me in therapy. "Are you young people really that busy during the summer?" she asked me. I was nodding. "Oh my," said Grützow; she smiled understandingly and went out.

I unpacked her computer and tried to decide whether the monitor would be better off on the left or right side of the desk. That's when I saw something lying on the surface of the desk—a green folder. And on the folder was the name Zulinski. I hesitated a bit too long, though, because as soon as I decided to reach for it, I heard footsteps approaching. Grützow came back into the room with a glass containing a pink drink. "For you." I took it and drank. It was raspberry juice, and it tasted gruesome.

"Left or right?" I asked.

"What?"

"The monitor. On the desk."

Grützow sat down on her chair and turned her head from left to right and from right to left again. She couldn't decide.

"I don't have much time," I said.

"When will you have time?"

"Whenever." We decided on Friday. To tell you the

truth, I would have preferred to help out tomorrow, since I want to know what's in those Zulinski papers. There surely can't be that many Zulinskis living around here.

D still hasn't shown up. What on earth's keeping her?

4:26 p.m. Sum total: 12. The sums total twelve, mostly. At least, more often than any other figure. Why, I don't know. Twelve is a nice number and a nice age. Much nicer than eleven or thirteen. I'm thirteen. For almost two weeks now. And my voice still hasn't changed. That is not so bad at twelve, but it is at thirteen. At thirteen, you're also supposed to have jumped from the 10-meter platform and kissed a girl. I haven't even been abroad.

D isn't coming. I'm not waiting any longer.

5:45 p.m. Sum total: 14. Holy Christmas! Mom's here.

I could tell already in the hallway. Unmistakably Mom's scent. That perfume with the slightly overripe fruit smell has got to be Mom. I'd recognize her even if she were wearing a new perfume. D told me a while ago that babies recognize their mothers by their scent. They don't recognize faces yet, but you can hold up a balloon in front of them with their mother's scent on it and they'll gurgle at it. I'm no longer a little baby, but I still recognize my mother by her scent.

Mom is here. The only question is, what's she doing here? She never comes without calling ahead of time. Her time's too valuable to just stop by, and the danger of there being nobody home is too great. The second question is: what should I do? Go in to see her and act like nothing's wrong? Has she already talked with Dad? If not, how did she get into the apartment? What does she know? Next to my bed is the stuffed elk that Sheryl dissected so lovingly. I've got to clear away that stuff. If Mom sees it, she'll think I'm crazy.

10:38 p.m. Sum total: 12. Twelve again. Could be that twelve is as dangerous as eleven. Could be that every sum is dangerous. I know exactly why I hate math.

Mom's sleeping in Dad's bed, even though she's not drunk. We just went down to the lake. Dad's still at work. Will he ever be surprised!

I know why twelve comes up so often. Because I'm always waiting to make sure that eleven doesn't come up. So it really is eleven that comes up. Like clockwork. It makes perfect sense to me.

I've lain down. The blanket is steamy warm, so I've tossed it aside.

This is what happened. Mom was sitting in the kitchen. She wasn't wearing a suit; instead she had on a red summer dress with thin straps. Next to Mom, Edda looks like dirt. I don't even want to talk about Mischka. "Victor," Mom said, and everything sounded normal, just as always. "How are you?"

"Good."

"Are you hungry? I went shopping."

There was an endless spread of food laid out on the table. Fresh rolls, tomatoes, cucumbers, radishes, a head of lettuce—the usual array of Mom's favorite veggies—

but also a container of chicken salad, sliced ham, baloney, a bar of almond chocolate, Swiss cheese, salmon,
two containers of pasta salad, and horseradish sauce.
There were jars of pickled herring and dill pickles, an
extra-spicy pepperoni, raspberry jam and blueberry jelly,
tomato preserves, two bottles of red wine, a giant bottle
of real Coke, two packages of banana mush, three pack-
ets of premium coffee, and two jars of apple butter. I
felt ill.

"No."

"But I am." And Mom began eating heartily. She ate—
not just what she always ate: slices of cucumbers, tomato
quarters, and leaves of lettuce—but two rolls stacked
with ham and Swiss cheese. Then she followed that with
sliced salmon she had smeared with horseradish sauce,
and after that some vanilla pudding with red berry sauce,
which I forgot to mention in my earlier list. I felt sicker
and sicker. Mom wasn't acting normal. I don't know how
long she ate.

"You're not saying a thing, Victor."

"What should I say?"

"How you are."

"I already said that. How are you, then?"

"Good."

"You see, you're not saying anything more either."

"I don't want to talk about me, but about you."

"There's nothing to talk about."

"Listen. Shall we go out for a little walk? It's easier to
talk when you're walking."

"Where, then?"

"To the lake. I haven't been there for an eternity."

I didn't want to go to the lake. But we went there anyway because I couldn't think of anyplace better to go. The lake is odd. I hate it, actually; I think it's eerie, but it possesses something that keeps drawing me back to it. Naturally, I took Mom to Kaiser Wilhelm's grave. I told her about his death. Mom hadn't known Kaiser Wilhelm at all. We sat on the bench, and gradually it grew dark. It was still warm, but a bit windy. I told Mom everything about Arnold, Mischka, and Edda. Also that Dad had thrown Edda out, because she talked too much about aliens and had sat on Mom's chair. "On *my* chair?" I explained that her place always had to remain empty. Mom looked quite startled at the news and didn't say another thing. Nor did I. I think both of us were startled. She had no idea, because she knew so little about how things were. And because she isn't here, also—that, too. But if *I* hadn't ever told her anything about it, that went triple for Dad.

Mom and I sat looking at each other. At that moment a strong blast of wind swept over us. It was quickly followed by another that ripped Mom's handbag from the bench. Mom jumped up. The trees above us were bending down almost to the ground, and Mom yelled, "Victor, we've got to get out of here!" That was easier said than done, because the storm prevented us from making much headway. Only between blasts of wind could we move along. "Where?" shouted Mom.

I had a pretty good idea. We couldn't possibly make it home before the serious storm let loose. But down by the harbor, there's a little stand that you can get under.

When I was little, I was always allowed to buy ice cream there. Dad and Mom used to stand for hours in front of a giant chessboard, contemplating each of their moves. I used to cross the chessboard—at first by tricycle, then with my bicycle (at first with training wheels, and then without them) and finally with in-line skates. Then Mom left; Dad had no one to play chess with, and I got bored with in-line skating. I haven't bought ice cream there since then. Now the stand isn't even open anymore, and the shutters are always rolled down and covered with graffiti.

We were caught by a few heavy raindrops, and then we reached the stand. Meanwhile, it had grown black as midnight. Mom was standing there, hugging herself and shivering. Tree limbs were coming down all around us, and the storm forced us back against the wall of the stand. The thunder and lightning were simultaneous, and when the lightning flashed, it wasn't just one flash, but five or six at the same time. After the flashes, it was even darker, because our eyes were blinded. Mom was holding her hand in front of her face. The rain came pelting in around the corners, and the roof helped shield us only a little.

At the next flash of lightning, I suddenly saw someone standing on the wharf out on the lake. In the middle of the rain; in the middle of the storm. The person was swaying and her hair was flapping. It was a girl. Mom saw her too. "She's going to get herself killed!" cried Mom.

Before I could say a word, Mom was off and running. In seconds, she was drenched. Mom stopped behind the girl and grabbed her by the shoulder. The girl was a head shorter than Mom and didn't respond to her. Mom was saying something and waving her hands in the air, but the girl stood there, unmoving. Suddenly, she made a move to bolt, but Mom was quicker and grabbed her. Mom was also stronger, and finally she came back to the kiosk, leading the girl by the arm. It was D.

Even the worst thunderstorm finally comes to an end, and when it had slowed to a drizzle, we set out for home. Mom didn't let go of D. "You're coming home with us until you've calmed down and have gotten dry." D went as limp as a wet washcloth next to Mom. Our hair was sopping and our shoes were squishing. There was no one out on the streets but us.

At home, Mom gave D some dry clothes of mine and asked her if she was hungry. D looked hungrily at the table full of food, but she shook her head.

"Deborah, where were you this afternoon?" I asked, but D didn't answer.

Mom looked at us, astounded. "You know each other?"

D still hadn't said anything, and I shut up too. Mom didn't know what she should do, so she slipped into the bathroom to get out of her wet clothes. Then D, who evidently had been waiting for the opportunity, jumped up from her chair, grabbed her backpack, and started to bolt. I tried to grab her, but I only caught her backpack, which turned over and spilled its contents.

"Leave me alone, you . . ."

Right then, Mom came back into the room in Dad's light blue bathrobe and grabbed D by the arm. "You stay here!"

"You can't order me around!"

"Yes, I can. You're staying here!"

"I've got to go home. My mother doesn't know where I am."

"We can call her."

"Let me go!"

"You can't go like that; you're wet to the bone."

"You're keeping me here against my will; I could have you arrested."

Mom had to laugh. That really threw D completely for a loop, and she began to crumble.

Meanwhile, I was scrambling around on the floor collecting D's stuff. A small red notebook, the dog collar, a bar of chocolate melted by the heat, a clothespin, two sour balls, a couple of eucalyptus cough drops, and her key chain. There was a figure hanging off the key chain, and it was an alien. It was the same one I had. I held it in my hand briefly, and then I tossed it into the knapsack with all the rest of the stuff.

Meanwhile, D was crying and crying down on the floor. Mom was being very gentle with her, and I thought to myself that it would have been better if she had had a girl instead of a boy. You can comfort girls so easily; they're more in touch with their feelings.

"What is the matter?" Mom asked after a while, and suddenly D began talking. Her dad had come home yesterday from America, to say goodbye. That's why she wanted to get home as quickly as possible. "He's got cancer, and he's only got a few days to live." D began crying again. Mom was completely shocked. Mom helped D stand up, and said, "I'll drive you back home to your apartment." D hesitated briefly, then began nodding. Then the two of them left. I don't know what to make of D's story.

Now both of them are gone. D didn't want me to ride along.

TUESDAY, AUGUST 6

Yesterday, I fell asleep on my journal. At some point, Mom must have come in and turned off the light. Now the sky is light blue. There are little clouds floating in it. Dad's come home from the night shift and was just in here. He hadn't known that Mom was here! He found her in his bed, asleep. Dad apologized for hitting me and began babbling about how bad the fares were, owing to last night's storm. Then he hung out in my room, looking somewhat lost; he didn't know where he should sleep, since he didn't trust himself to get into bed with Mom. I told him he could sleep in my room.

Now he's asleep in my bed and I'm sitting in the kitchen with my journal and watching TV. The storm killed eleven people in Germany. Eleven once again. Seven died when trees fell on them, three were drowned in an underground garage, and one had a heart attack out of fear.

* * *

Dammit, dammit, what's wrong with D? Mom's just walked into the kitchen in Dad's bathrobe and asked, "Hasn't Paul gotten home yet?"

"Sure," I say, "he's asleep."

"But where is he sleeping?"

"In my bed."

"What did he say?"

"About what?"

"About my being here."

"Nothing. Only that he didn't know where he should sleep."

"Nothing?"

"Oh, well. He was a bit surprised."

"Nothing more?"

"No."

"Victor, turn off the TV."

I've switched the channel as we've been talking, to the children's station. I click off the remote control. I know Mom hates that. First, TV in the morning and second, leaving the TV on but not watching it. It's as bad as leaving it on, she insists. But today she hasn't said anything about it. She's sliced open a roll, put a little horseradish sauce and a few slices of cucumber on it. She's drunk a glass of tap water with it. "The bad weather killed eleven people in all of Germany," I say. Mom looks up briefly from her roll. "I'm not surprised," she says.

"Don't you think it's awful? Eleven's a lot."

"Yes, yes. Eleven is awful." Mom doesn't seem to care about the bad weather. She waves her water glass back and forth. "Has Dad said anything?"

"No. Just that the storm was bad for business."

Mom sits there thinking and winds a strand of hair around her finger. Sometimes, when she's sitting here at the kitchen table, I get the feeling that she hasn't been away for a single day.

"Mom, do you think some numbers have a special significance?"

"Numbers?"

"Well, yeah . . . eleven, for instance."

"Eleven? Of course not." Then Mom begins laughing. "Some people maintain that twenty-three has a special significance. But the only people who do are conspiracy theorists."

"What are conspiracy theorists?"

"They're people who believe that the world is run by a bunch of secret societies and that everything is controlled by them."

"Could aliens be in that kind of secret group?"

"Why are you asking me about aliens? Dad's the star freak here."

"I can still ask you if you believe in aliens, can't I?"

"If you want to know the truth, Victor, I do believe in aliens. Somewhere in this gigantic universe there's got to be other intelligent life besides us. It would be really preposterous to suppose that we were the only ones. But I don't think those beings are trying to take over Earth." Mom seems not to have slept much. She says, "Your little girlfriend there is pretty spacey. And she didn't want to say anything about herself."

I explain to Mom that D's lost her dog and that I've

gotten to know her at the swimming pool. "But she's not my girlfriend. I barely know her."

"I didn't mean it that way."

Now this conversation is getting somewhere. "It's a pretty nice block of apartment buildings where Deborah lives, isn't it?" I say.

"Buildings?" Mom asks. "Deborah doesn't live in an apartment building. She lives in a very nice one-family house with a large garden."

Mom bites into her horseradish roll. While she's chewing, she slices a tomato into quarters.

"Mom, are you blind? Deborah doesn't live in a nice one-family house."

"Listen, Victor, I ought to know where I drove Deborah to."

"And where was that?"

"Earl Street, number seventeen."

Then I have to laugh, even though I'm not finding it at all amusing. On the contrary. Something pretty haywire is going on here. "Deborah lives in Kimbernstrasse. Kimbernstrasse, number eleven." And at that, Mom doesn't know what to say; neither do I.

D's obviously pulled the wool completely over Mom's eyes. I'm really pissed at D, and I'm sure Mom will be at least as annoyed. But Mom just sits there on her chair, forgets her food, and says, "Do you have a map?" I have to laugh again, and say, "The map's sleeping in my bed right now." And I can't for the life of me stop laughing; I feel like I'm going to suffocate. The bad weather hasn't really cooled things down, and you can almost see the water vapor in the air in the kitchen. I go onto the balcony. None of this is any fun. Mom comes out after me. We look down into the yard. The oak tree has lost some of its branches, and the superintendent is collecting the debris down below. Mom puts her arm around my shoulder. "If you want to know the truth, everything about Deborah struck me as a bit odd. And what's with this story about her father?"

I'm about to tell Mom more about it when Dad walks out onto the balcony and says, "Victor, with all the racket you make, how is it that you ever get a minute of sleep?"

Mom turns toward Dad and says, "Paul!"

And Dad says, "Christine."

Mom and Dad look at each other, and I suddenly feel a little superfluous. I wriggle my way past the two of them and buzz off. I knew it. The two of them still love each other. A million years from now, they'll still be in love.

Then I go look up Earl Street on the Internet. Earl Street is pretty much exactly where D doesn't live; it's the ritzy part of town. You might guess that just by the name of the street. *Earl* Street! But the theory only goes so far. Dad says most of the swells live in Kaiser Street. He drives his fares there all the time.

What I really want to do is go to Earl Street right now, but I'm sure D isn't there anymore. Who knows where she's hiding? Earl Street isn't that far away from the lake. I think that story about her father was just made up; it was only a trick to gain Mom's sympathy.

Mom and Dad lounge around in the kitchen and talk and talk. Because I want to do something, I go downstairs to fetch the mail. Leaning in the entryway is a mattress and the African mask. Four boxes are stacked one on top of the other. A man in white overalls and a checked shirt is in front of the door. He has put down two colored buckets beside him and is studying the doorbell listings.

"Haberlach. Have I got the right place?" asks the man.

"You want Edda Haberlach? Ms. Haberlach lives on the third floor," I say. "Did you ring her buzzer?"

"Of course. It's what you do when you want to see someone."

The man keeps pushing the button, but of course nothing happens. No hum, no buzz, no "hello" through the intercom. At that moment, I hear hurried footsteps, and then Edda is standing beside me. Of course it isn't Edda, but she looks like Edda. At least the hair and the face. It's Edda's double from the streetcar.

"Is Edda leaving?" I ask.

"You can see for yourself." The woman picks up the African mask and ignores me.

"Are you Edda's sister?"

"Yes, her twin. And you've got to be Victor, the one who's been terrorizing the whole building with your letters. Edda had a nervous breakdown because of them."

"I didn't write those letters," I say, and go out walking. It's been a while.

Back at home. I want to think, and so I've closed my journal. You can think better without any distractions, but I haven't been able to think, only stare into space. And so I'm looking at the cover of my shiny, 3-D, silver-patterned journal. I can see my face reflected in it. It's broken up into many pieces because of the silver pattern. Like a mosaic. I hardly recognize myself. Clouds are floating past my window. Fluffy white and harmless against the light blue, although they don't look like they've forgotten yesterday's storm. They're just hanging around and waiting to change their form and get into trouble. I've got to do something.

Maybe Mom will stay forever. She hasn't stayed here overnight since she left, except for those couple of hours. And she's never worn a red summer dress here. Besides that, she's never *not* brought a present with her. I mean, she brought something this time as well—about ten pounds of food—but up till now, she's always brought something especially for *me*. Almost as if she were apologizing that she couldn't spend time with me; as if she were sorry that she wasn't living here anymore. This business with the food looks more like she wants to stay.

I've got the feeling that everything's falling into place for everyone else. Mischka and Arnold seem happy to have found each other. Mom's come back to Dad, and Edda's finally been accounted for. Only my life is getting more chaotic. But I think D's the only one who's causing all the chaos.

I can't get her out of my head. I can't just hang out here in my room forever, looking at the sky and seeing my reflection in my 3-D, silver-patterned journal. Of course, I could go looking for D, but that seems futile. And looking for a dog like Contessa seems even harder.

It could have wound up in almost anyone's Crock-Pot. I doubt that'll ever happen to D.

I've got a better idea. I'm going to write a letter to Mischka and Arnold. One that will tell them that it wasn't me.

> *Hi, Mischka! Hi, Arnold!*
> *I don't think it's very nice of you to suspect me of having written the letters. I got some myself, you know. All right, I know that's no proof. I did scrounge around in Mischka's apartment, and I did release the flies. That wasn't right. But honestly, I was only trying to find the letter writer. If you want, you can go to the police; I wouldn't blame you. At least they'll quickly find out that I didn't have anything to do with the letters.*
> *With best wishes,*
> *Victor Forlands*

The letter's in my journal. I'm not going to send it, even though it cost me some effort to type it on Dad's old typewriter. I typed it with the machine because I wanted to prove that our typewriter types completely differently from the one belonging to the letter writer.

It took me about an hour to complete the few sentences,

and I had to keep rolling in fresh paper because I was constantly making mistakes. I wanted to slip it under Mischka's door, but I didn't, because I suddenly thought, Then they'll all *really* think I was the one. Because only the perpetrator would be too cowardly to stand before the victim and look him in the eye. That's why the letter's here in my book. The typewriter's sitting like a nasty black animal on my desk.

I'm back at the lake. As I figure it, there are only two places where I might be able to find either Contessa, or D, or both of them. Those are the lake and Kennedy Square. Of course, that's utter nonsense—they could be almost anywhere in this bloody town. Or even out of this town, out of the country, out of this universe. Anywhere at all.

I'm sitting on the dock, exactly where D was standing yesterday. What did she want here? Surely not to throw herself in? That would be completely senseless; D is a supergood swimmer. Did she hope to be struck by lightning? That's even less likely than guessing all six numbers in the lottery. At any rate, that's what Dad always said when I got afraid of a thunderstorm.

The grass is wet, and there are brown leaves lying around. It looks autumnal, but the air's so heavy you're almost drowning. The dog days are not over yet.

There behind the stand, I see Arnold. He isn't alone. But I can't recognize who he's with.

I don't believe it! The dog days are definitely not over; they're only just beginning!

Okay, there was a woman with Arnold. The woman was

Mischka. That didn't surprise me; you can tell that something's been going on between them. But besides her, there was also a dog, and the dog was a red cocker spaniel. It looked like Kaiser Wilhelm, but it was Contessa. Completely unbelievable. But it was; I know Contessa. She's got a kink in her tail, and when you call her she wags her head.

Arnold naturally wasn't calling her Contessa; he was calling her Daisy, and he was surprised that she wasn't responding to that stupid name. She had even snapped at him a couple of times.

I followed the three of them. They walked around the lake and held hands. Well, not all three of them; Contessa was on a leash, but Arnold and Mischka were very affectionate. And shortly before the Lakeside Café, they even kissed. I was following them at a pretty fair distance, so that Contessa couldn't scent me.

Then the two of them entered the café and sat themselves down on the terrace. Arnold ordered a bowl of ice cream with cherries and a paper parasol, and Mischka ordered raspberry cake with cream. I was watching the two of them through the hedge and trying to catch snippets of their conversation. The two of them weren't talking much, however; they were mostly preoccupied with eating. Arnold was feeding Contessa the cherries.

"I'd be careful with those cherries," Mischka said.

"Dogs need vitamins too."

"But not alcohol. Those cherries were pickled in rum." Mischka sniffed at Arnold's ice cream bowl.

"Maybe she'll like 'Daisy' a little better if she's tipsy. Daisy! Daisy, come to Daddy!"

"She's not responding to 'Daisy.' I wonder what her name is? Come to think of it, where did you get Daisy?"

"Off the Internet. From a dealer."

"I'd never buy a living creature off the Internet."

"Why not? You've got to use modern technology."

"I don't know. Who knows, it could be the dog was taken by a dognapper."

"How do you figure that?"

"Because she behaves so oddly." Mischka was trying to stroke Contessa, but I could hear Contessa growling.

"She just doesn't know me. That's normal. The dealer said the previous owners hadn't been especially nice to Daisy."

"And you believed it?"

"Why not?"

6:06 p.m. Sum total: 12. No one's at home. Not a trace of Mom or Dad. I called D's number, but it was constantly busy. So I wrote another letter. It was to D:

> *Hello, Deborah.*
>
> *I hope you get this letter. It's important. You see, I've found Contessa again. This time for real. It's not a trick or a trap. She's really here, and she's doing well under the circumstances. The circumstances are that Arnold has*

her now. So Contessa is
living here in the build-
ing. He bought her off the
Internet from a dealer.
I suggest a neutral
meeting place. Tomorrow
morning at ten in Kennedy
Square.
Until then,
Victor

I needed more time for this letter than I did for the other. I had to worry over each word at least five times, and the typewriter clanged more and more rebelliously each time I rolled a new sheet of paper into it. First, I was going to simply drop the letter into a mailbox and let the postal system deliver it, but then D would only get the letter the day after tomorrow. So now I'm going to climb into the streetcar and deliver it to her in person. No, even better; I'm going to slip it under her door. I've also left a note for Mom and Dad on the kitchen table. Like D's letter, I wrote it on the typewriter. That way, bit by bit, I'll get better at it.

Hello, Mom. Hello, Dad.
I've just stepped out
for a bit and will be back
around ten-thirty. Don't
worry.
Victor

11:08 p.m. Sum total: 10. It took me longer than I expected, because I was stopped by Bombs Away as I was leaving the light blue apartment building. I saw only the glowing tip of his cigarette.

"What're you hanging around here for?" He was holding me firmly by the sleeve.

"It's none of your business," I said, and shook him off.

"Everything's my business." Bombs Away blew cigarette smoke in my face. "What're you lookin' for here?"

"Nothing."

Bombs Away grabbed my arm and forced it behind me. "Don't lie. Or you'll be lookin' for your arm in the trash."

"I'm looking for Deborah."

"Very funny. Who's that supposed to be?" Bombs Away forced my arm up higher.

"The red-haired girl with the cocker spaniel and the buggy."

Bombs Away didn't release me.

My arm had been broken at least three times by this point. "No one named Deborah lives here. Now repeat after me, 'I won't show my face around here anymore.' "

"Bite me."

"Say it!"

"Bite me!"

I got a kick in the shins. It was no use. I repeated the sentence. Mom and Dad still haven't gotten back. I'm going to sleep.

WEDNESDAY, AUGUST 7

There was a baloney sandwich lying in the kitchen. All the jars and packages that Mom had brought were still on top of the kitchen table. Someone had stuck the perishable things in the refrigerator. The refrigerator was more full than I'd ever seen it in my life. But I wondered why there was a baloney sandwich lying there. The baloney sandwich meant Dad got home late last night. Alone. If he were with Mom, he'd never eat a baloney sandwich at night. He also wouldn't just leave it lying around half eaten, because Mom would definitely find that unappetizing.

I crept into Dad's bedroom. Dad was lying there. Like a sausage with a face. With a happy, sleepy face. He was alone. Mom wasn't there, and the other side of the bed didn't look like anyone had been lying in it. I was going to close the bedroom door quietly, but Dad woke up. "Victor?"

"Where's Mom?"

"Mom left last night."

"But . . . I thought she was going to stay."

That wasn't what I wanted to say at all.

"Me too, Victor. Me too," Dad said, and his sleepy face

was no longer happy, but sad. He sat up in bed. His face grew even sadder, until it was so sad that a tear rolled out of his left eye. "Victor, come here."

I went over, but not too near. I didn't want to feel as sad as Dad.

"Victor, I really thought she was going to stay . . . at least for a little while."

"She didn't say goodbye to me."

"You weren't here."

"She could have waited."

"Oh, you know Mom. She doesn't wait. She won't wait, ever. . . . Not on her life, if that's what it takes." Then another tear rolled out of Dad's right eye.

"I thought she was going to stay, because she'd never worn a red summer dress here before," I said.

Dad pulled himself together at the mention of the red summer dress. "Victor, I've got to sleep a bit more. I drove a long time. Wake me, if you think of it."

I didn't know whether or not I'd think of it.

Now I've got to get going, to Kennedy Square. Will Deborah show up?

9:47 a.m. It's going to be hot again today.

I'm sitting on a bench, thinking about the sum totals. For the last time, I swear. I've worked up some statistics. The grand champ for sum totals is twelve. It's shown up four times; eleven's shown up twice. Three, ten, thirteen, fourteen, sixteen, seventeen, and eighteen have each come up once. The smallest sum total you could ever come up with is zero, and that's because of midnight—

00:00. The greatest possible sum total would be twenty-three, and you'd reach that at 9:59 p.m.—one minute before ten. Now, I could, of course, work up which sum total is greatest out of the whole day, from a purely statistical standpoint, but that borders on work, and it would take me at least half a day to do. Maybe I'll do it if I get totally bored. But definitely not now, even though there's nothing happening here at Kennedy Square.

Contessa. I've been staring at that word now for a quarter of an hour. The posters that D distributed and hung up here are lying around in tatters in the mud. Some of the posters are lying facedown; you can read the writing on them, but in reverse. At first, I was looking at the posters without thinking. It took me fifteen minutes to get it. If you read "Contessa" backward, you get the word "assetnoC." Asset-noc!

My brain has shut down. I can't seem to grasp this information. D will be here soon. I hope.

D's not showing up. I'm going.

D isn't Deborah; D is Dagmar!

All right—first things first. Around eleven o'clock, I was out in front of our building without my key. I didn't want to buzz Dad; Dad's too miserable, and I didn't want to add to his misery. Just as I was about to go back out wandering, Mrs. von Grützow walked up and said, "Hello, Victor." She even pronounced my name correctly for the first time. "What's wrong, Victor? You look like a cat's walked over your grave."

"A cat?"

"Oh, of course, I mean a rat."

"A thousand rats, at least."

"You want to come visit me? I'll give you a snack."

Another serving of that horrible drink? But the idea of visiting Mrs. von Grützow was all right. Better than any other idea I had. I offered to help her with her computer, and she thought that was a good idea. My mood was improving; I was pretty curious about that folder titled "Zulinski."

I didn't die from the drink; this time it was blueberry and cranberry juice mixed together, but at least Mrs. von Grützow had put ice cubes in it. She retreated into the next room with a notebook and a couple of files. "Taxes," she said with a heavy sigh.

The Zulinski file was still on the desk in her office. I'd have preferred to dive into it immediately, but first I had to feign a little zeal. So I started off by laying down the system cables and hooking a few things up. The truth is, I wasn't sure about any of it; I've never done it before. I once installed a couple of game consoles, but never a whole system with drives and all the accessories. I spread out all the manuals and CDs over and around the Zulinski file, and in between reading the directions from the monitor, I managed to page through quite a bit of it. I didn't understand a lot of it, because I couldn't make out the many abbreviations and technical terms. What a *baaaaaad* scrawl Mrs. von Grützow has! My penmanship is beautiful in comparison. But here's the most important thing I discovered: D's name isn't Deborah; it's Dagmar.

Dagmar Zulinski was born August 11 here in the city. She's my age. Her mother works for a mail-order shipping company and has a drinking problem. Her father's unknown. The father of her sister comes and goes and gets into trouble. When her mother's drunk, D has to take care of her sister by herself. D has been sent to a psychologist, because she cuts school and has been terrorizing her fellow students and teachers with anonymous letters.

So if I've worked this all out correctly, D wrote the letters we've been getting. To tell you the truth, that didn't surprise me very much. After I had discovered that stuff about Contessa and Asset-noc, it had actually become clear to me. I just hadn't really admitted it to myself. Despite that, I still have no idea *why* D had written letters to strangers in a strange building. Besides, I simply can't believe she'd come up with an idea that twisted all on her own. She must have gotten the idea from somewhere else!

4:46 p.m. I've spread my towel out on the lawn. The swimming pool is jammed full of people; up on the 5- and 7.5-meter diving platforms, they're jostling one another and acting cool. If I wait another half hour, the lifeguard will open the 10-meter platform. The lifeguard will stand up on the 7.5-meter platform and make sure that the water below is empty and that only one person at a time walks out and jumps. Without a running start. When you're up there, there's no more hiding. You've got to go off.

I'll do that today. I'll do it without the witch. I don't need her at all. And besides, I imagine she's also the one responsible for Kaiser Wilhelm's death; I just have a hunch. D seems capable of anything. She must have spied on our whole building; otherwise, she'd never have been able to write letters like that. She must be crazy. And I'm still searching for her to help her out! I'm a complete fool. She's been playing me for an idiot. Playing the master detective and telling me stories of espionage and detection, and proposing totally idiotic theories about aliens. And all this time, she's been writing the letters herself.

It's just unbelievable. And everyone's been suspecting me. D is a witch; I've known it right from the start, and that's not the half of it: she's a super-mega-bossy witch.

Today, I'll jump from the 10-meter platform. And that dork, Lukas, will just look at me and say nothing once he's come back from America.

They can all bite me. The whole lot of them, everybody: Dad, Mom, D, Arnold, Mischka, Edda, her odd sister, the aliens . . .

Bombs Away can bite me too. As my idiot luck would have it, I put my towel down right by him and his clique. I didn't realize it at first, because they weren't at their towels. I lay on my back for a while and was thinking of this and that when I suddenly heard his voice near me. I put my arm over my face and was hoping that he wouldn't recognize me.

"Look, it's the baby face."

That was Bombs Away's voice.

"Who?"

"That one who's always hanging around my building. Hey, baby face, who told you you could put your towel down next to us?"

"I can lie down where I want to," I said from behind my arm.

"You mouthin' off to me or what?"

I didn't move and thought fearfully of yesterday evening.

"What do you want with Daggi? Why're you spying on her?"

I shut up, and stayed on my back, and kept staring at the back of my arm.

Bombs Away moved closer. "You can poke your nose in any goddamn pool in this town, but not here. You've got one minute to get lost." He blew his cigarette smoke into my face. "I'm counting. . . ."

It was all just too much. I got up, grabbed my stuff, and left. Behind me, I could hear his mean laughter.

Strictly speaking, the swimming pool is now off limits to me. And I was going to jump off the 10-meter. . . . But the worst thing is, D has disappeared. And the absolute worst is that I care. D is someone I can take or leave. After all, all she is, is a super-mega-bossy witch with a super-mega attitude.

When I get home around seven, Dad's sitting in the kitchen. He's off today. His brow is furrowed like corduroy. That means trouble. He's holding a letter in his hands. "You should never open letters. Never, never, never." By now, I've almost come to agree with him.

"What's the letter?"

"They're raising the rent."

"On what?" I ask like an idiot.

"On the apartment."

"Huh."

"Victor, the matter's serious. With this much of a rent increase, we can't stay here another month."

"Well, you're the one who wanted to leave."

"Victor!"

At that moment, the doorbell starts ringing.

"Open the door, Victor."

Obediently, I go to the door. It's Arnold and Mischka. They want to see Dad. I think it's another meeting of conspirators, but they're not keeping anything under wraps. Mischka and Arnold, who now appear not to go anywhere unless they go together, also got letters about rent hikes. Contessa greets me wildly, and I stroke her soft coat. So it really is Contessa.

The adults spread themselves out in the kitchen. I make coffee for them and listen. They're talking about a renters' association and about shamelessness and filthy capitalists. I leave the kitchen, since I can't shake the idea that they'll talk more freely when I'm not around. But when I eavesdrop at the door, they're still talking about filthy capitalists and no sense of shame and rent strikes. Adults really sometimes do go on and on. I'm about to head to my bedroom when Arnold suddenly starts in on the anonymous letters.

"What about the anonymous letters?" asks Mischka.

Dad says something to the effect that "That's just water under the bridge. Shouldn't we be glad that nastiness has stopped?"

"N-n-no. I f-f-feel the I-I-I-I-I..." Arnold seems to be pretty upset.

"Arnold, calm down."

There's a pause, during which Arnold breathes heavily. Then he takes a deep breath. "The anonymous letters have something to d-d-do with the rent h-h-hikes."

"Like what?"

"The owner wants to get rid of us."

"C'mon, Arnold. You're just fantasizing," growls Dad. From where I'm listening, he's hardest to understand because he always mumbles when he's in a bad mood.

Mischka says, "But maybe he's right. They do want to get rid of us. The apartments here are much too inexpensive."

"Too inexpensive?" Dad laughs. "I can't afford to pay one more cent."

"Still, the apartments here are cheap. The owner is old, and for years he's forgotten to raise the rents. Now his children are on the scene. And they want to renovate the building and make it into lofts. Can you imagine how many units they could convert this place into?"

Dad grunts.

"Yes. P-p-precisely. They've already driven Edda out. And that's the reason they p-poisoned K-K-Kaiser Wilhelm."

"What? Edda's not living here anymore?" Dad was still catching up with the news of Edda's departure.

"Edda has left," Arnold explains.

"And here we were blaming poor Victor for writing those letters," Mischka says. "He could never have engineered something like this."

They haven't got a clue! But I'm still kind of glad that I've received their forgiveness, and that I'm the only one who already knows what's happening. I disappear into my room with Contessa.

I take out the Polaroid camera and take a photo of her. I've gotten an idea, you see, and I'm going to send D the snapshot. Then maybe she'll call me. Because of the letters and the three-ring circus she's set in motion, I'm pretty pissed at her, but then when I stop and think about it, I get a pretty crappy feeling. Something is really wrong with D. Sometimes I'm afraid she might do something. Something really bad. I've got to find her.

Finally, I put the snapshot into an envelope and write D's address on it so it can be sent through the mail. That way, I won't have to encounter Bombs Away again. Maybe D will finally respond!

Then I go back into the kitchen, where the adults are still talking. Mischka has moved to the stove and is busying herself with pots and pans. All Dad says is "Victor, it's eleven o'clock, you've got to go to bed." Mischka says, "Wouldn't you like something to eat?"

I shake my head. "I've already brushed my teeth." One of the best excuses ever.

Mischka says, "We'll be sure to save you some casserole." Then I get another bright idea and I say, "Hey, Arnold, where did you actually get Daisy? She looks like Kaiser Wilhelm."

"I b-b-bought her; wh-wh-what else?"

"At a pet store?"

"N-n-no, off the Internet."

"I've heard that dognappers sell on the Internet."

"Now, don't you start with that. That's what Mischka's been saying."

"Could be true, couldn't it?"

Arnold opens his mouth to say something. He's obviously not certain anymore that everything about Daisy is on the up and up.

"Well, it doesn't matter," I say. "But can I take her out walking, maybe? I mean, when you don't have the time?"

"Sure, you can do that."

THURSDAY, AUGUST 8

8:37 a.m. There's a gigantic pot with unknown contents on top of the stove, and the odor of garlic is poisoning the air. I've fought my way through it and out onto the balcony by holding my breath. It's hot outside, and the light is hazy. Not a leaf is stirring. This is my last summer here. Next year, we'll be living somewhere else. I'm not especially sad about it. Time for a change. And maybe we'll even furnish the next apartment properly!

It's 78.8 degrees Fahrenheit outside; 72.6 degrees inside. I know this because Dad's bought a digital thermometer with display readings for both indoors and outdoors.

* * *

11:48 a.m. I'm not going to let the pool stay off limits to me. Bombs Away is not usually there in the mornings. Still, I put my towel down somewhere else for safety's sake. I jump off the 7.5-meter platform three times, and five times off the 5-meter platform.

But the pool irritates me. I want to think, but it's too hot. The heat's frying my brain, and the little sea horses on my towel are jumping around like crazy. I've had this towel for as long as I've been alive, I think. One stripe is blue with a red sea horse, and the other is red with a white sea horse. I always used to imagine that the red sea horse on the blue background was Dad and the white sea horse on the red background was Mom. In the bright light they keep shifting around. They're shimmering like crazy, and they want to make me crazy too.

Dad's an old fart! When I came home just now, he was sitting in the kitchen as usual, reading the paper. He said, "They've found an antidote to the botulin toxin."

I said, "Oh my."

"Do you even know what the botulin toxin is?"

"No."

"*Clostridium botulinum* is the most deadly poison in the world. A gram of it could kill a million people."

"Oh my."

"Victor."

"Yes."

"Doesn't that interest you?"

"Not a whole lot."

"Victor. Don't you at least know what an antidote is?"

"Nah."

"Victor. You've studied Latin. Put your three brain cells together."

"They're otherwise engaged. Besides, I'm phlegmatic, remember?"

"An antidote is used to counteract poison. And it comes from 'anti,' which means 'against.'"

"I know all that." Dad doesn't know any Latin. He only knows that "anti" means "against" from crossword puzzles. I asked him, "Then what's the meaning of 'dote'?"

"Don't ask stupid questions." I was pretty sure Dad hadn't a clue what "dote" meant. But that was also irrelevant, since he went back to leafing through his paper. Finally, he said, "Someone called for you."

"Who?"

"I don't know. Some girl. She left a message on the machine."

But there wasn't anything on the machine. I had just played it back. Dad had erased it. Evidently by accident. I was pissed. "And what did the girl say?"

"Something crazy. That she wanted to see you, and that it was urgent, and that you should go somewhere at some time."

"Somewhere sometime? Didn't she get more exact than that?"

"Of course . . . but I forgot."

I yelled at Dad. I screeched at him as if I were a little boy. He crumbled beneath my words, his eyes startled. I was awful.

"Victor. I'm sorry. It was an accident."

"Nice accident," I shot back, and left, slamming the kitchen door behind me and leaving my poor father sitting there with his paper.

To tell the truth, I had no idea what to do. No one was home at the Zulinskis', and no one answered D's stupid cell phone. What does she have the thing for, if she doesn't use it?

I looked in the encyclopedia. "Antidote" isn't Latin at all; it's Greek, and it comes from "antidoton" and means quite simply "against poison." You can't believe everything that comes out of Dad's mouth.

Now I'm going to go to D's place in Kimbernstrasse and put the snapshot under her door. If I send it by mail, it'll take until tomorrow to get there. She's got to come home sometime. I'll give her one more chance to call me.

Since I'm putting my life in danger going to Kimbernstrasse, I've gone to the drugstore and bought sunglasses and a sun hat to disguise myself. That way, if I encounter Bombs Away, at least he won't recognize me right off. I also bought a 1.5-liter bottle of real Coke, for energy, and took a big swig of it.

3:46 p.m. It is unbelievably humid; there's hardly a breath of air stirring. I'm hunkered down in the rain shelter at the streetcar stop, keeping an eye on D's apartment building. I'm sweating under the sun hat. The cola has gotten warm. There's nothing going on at the building; it's like it's dead.

Maybe we'll get another thunderstorm.

Around five o'clock, I approached the apartment building. Late afternoon is a good time. At that time, Bombs Away is most likely at the pool terrorizing the other divers.

I rang all the doorbells once again, but nobody buzzed me in. Keyless, I stood there at the front door for a bit, until I heard someone coming up behind me. I turned around, and it was a woman with a blubbering kid in a stroller. She turned the key in the door, and I held it for her. She immediately shoved the kid into my arms and said, "Can you carry the little one up for me?" The kid was drooling on my T-shirt. "Fourth floor, left," the woman yelled behind me, and began to follow with her groceries.

I did look a little strange in my hat and sunglasses as I trudged up the stairwell. I hoped Bombs Away wouldn't suddenly turn up! As a precaution, I pulled my hat down lower over my face. But the kid didn't like that at all and grabbed my hat away and—with it—my sunglasses. They fell on the floor and broke. By that time, the mother had made it up the stairs and was gasping. "Jessica!" she shrilled, and wobbled over to me. "Did she break your glasses?" I nodded. "It's not a big deal," I murmured, although I thought it was a big deal, because I had now lost my disguise.

"Such a nice, helpful young man," she murmured. "You could certainly teach my son a thing or two. But the whole summer he's off with his buddies at the pool, jumping off the high platform." The woman went on, "This morning, I sent him off to do the shopping, and he used all the money for a pair of pants. For a pair of pants that were all tattered and hanging off his butt. The kid bought a worn-out pair of pants, can you believe it? But do you think he'll help his mother around the house?" The woman sighed. "You don't live here, do you? I've never seen you before."

"No." I'd gotten nervous. It had just occurred to me that I was probably talking to Bombs Away's mother! No, I was certain of it.

"Oh, do me a favor and carry the little one into the apartment, and keep her occupied while I put away this stuff. She's so quiet with you."

The little one *was* quiet in my arms. I had already gotten very handy with Sheryl. "Would you like a glass of Coke?" The woman had taken a gigantic bottle of Coke out of the refrigerator and was offering it to me. "With ice?"

I nodded.

"It's hot as blazes today. There'll definitely be another storm. You come to visit someone here?"

"I'd like to," I answered, "but there's nobody answering at the Zulinskis."

The woman eyed me suspiciously for a moment and then asked, "What do you want with the Zulinskis?"

"I've found a dog, one that I'm sure belongs to D. Zulinski."

"A dog? A red cocker spaniel?"

"Yes. Contessa is the name on the collar."

"Contessa! Well, at least that's some good news."

"What's happened?"

The woman didn't answer my question but instead asked me, "And where is the dog?"

"At my place. I thought I'd leave her there, since nobody answered the phone...."

"Uh-huh...well, talk's cheap."

I took the envelope out of my backpack and held the snapshot out to the woman. "That's Contessa, isn't it?"

The woman gazed at the picture for a second and nodded.

"And how can I reach the Zulinskis?" I asked.

"You can't."

"What do you mean?"

The woman looked at me for a bit and said nothing. "Oh, well, I might as well tell you, since you don't know the family. Ms. Zulinski had to go into the hospital. She drank herself half dead again."

"And Deb...Dagmar?" I stammered.

"How do you know Daggi?"

"Her name was on the dog collar" was the only thing I was able to come up with as an explanation.

"I'd have offered to take her in, because she stays here more than she does at home, but that won't work out. She's had to go live with relatives she can't stand... oh!...but now you've reminded me that I've got to go play florist at the Zulinskis'. In this heat, the plants need water every day. It'd be nice if you could carry the little one. She has to go where I do. And you've got a kind heart, she can tell."

Then we went down to the third floor, and I saw D's apartment for the first time. It was tiny and pretty messy. There were a kitchen, a living room, and a children's room with two beds. A couple of things struck me immediately.

There were a whole slew of dog books on the bookshelf, and the whole room was papered with posters of dogs. On the desk there was a typewriter. Not a black one, like Dad's, but one made of light gray plastic. There was paper on the floor. I recognized it immediately. It was *the* paper.

"Daggi's just crazy for dogs," the woman said abruptly as she came into the bedroom with the watering can. "I think she worries about that mutt more than she does about her mother. That dog meant everything to her. She wants to be a dog breeder. No kidding, she has plans. One time she found this male cocker spaniel, somewhere in the city, in some old house she said was just like a castle. She said she wanted to live there. I said to her, 'Daggi, what's with you? The people who live there have *money*.' Well, anyway, in this house she was always talking about, there was a male cocker spaniel. And she wanted him to breed Contessa. You know, Contessa is a purebred, and she said the male cocker spaniel also had a pedigree. She wound up hanging around outside that house the whole afternoon hoping to catch that dog. 'Hey, do you know what a cocker spaniel pup will bring?' she said to me."

The woman was now through watering the plants, which all looked a little dried out. We went back upstairs. "And then?" I asked.

"How should I know?"

In the meantime, we'd gotten back into her kitchen and the woman had taken peanut butter crackers out of a cupboard. She shook them into a gold-rimmed bowl decorated with a lady in a crinoline holding a parasol. The lady disappeared under the crackers. I didn't care for any crackers; your mouth gets so dry from them, but the woman kept saying, "In this heat, you've got to watch your salt intake. Dig in!" and I didn't dare refuse.

"Maybe you could just bring the dog over here? Daggi can't keep her while she's with her relatives, and I'd love to look after her," the woman proposed.

"But wouldn't it make Daggi happy to see the dog? I mean, I could just arrange to meet her?" The woman didn't seem terribly enthusiastic about my idea, but finally she gave me the address and telephone number of the relatives.

Suddenly, the only thing I wanted was to get out of there. I quickly said goodbye.

Outside, it was thundering.

FRIDAY, AUGUST 9

8:12 a.m. Contessa's sitting in our backyard. I don't understand Arnold at all. Why does he have a dog when he's too lazy to walk it? Kaiser Wilhelm died in that backyard. Who knows, maybe the yard is contaminated or someone's put rat poison out. The owner, for instance.

Because he doesn't like dogs or something. Or because he wants to get rid of us. Rat poison is deadly. And it's a very painful death, I'm told. As I'm thinking about that and considering what other kinds of poison there might be in the yard, Arnold shows up. "Hello, Victor!"

"Hello, Arnold."

Arnold wants to take Contessa back upstairs with him. That's my opportunity. "Hey, Arnold, don't you think it would do Contessa some good to go for a walk?"

"Contessa?"

"Oops. I mean Daisy, of course. You know, I keep thinking she's Contessa, the redheaded girl's dog."

"Oh, her." Arnold picks his nose. "What was she doing hanging around here?"

"She was visiting me."

"But I've seen her around here many times without you. For weeks and weeks."

"Weeks and weeks?"

"Yes, yes." Arnold is still occupied with his nose, and his thoughts seem to be somewhere else entirely.

I say, "I don't want to get into it, and of course, it's your dog, but Kaiser Wilhelm already died here in the backyard, and I don't know if it's a good idea for Daisy to be sitting around so much down here."

"Wh-wh-what do you mean?"

"I've been thinking that maybe someone put out poison. Rat poison, for instance. Trying to get rid of you."

"Hmmm."

"And then I was thinking that I could take your dog for a walk, if you've got too much to do right now."

"V-V-Victor, you're a good kid. You think of everything."

"So, may I take Daisy?"

"That'd really be a big help."

I am not a good kid at all. Because Arnold is going to miss his dog soon.

10:17 a.m. I called D's relatives. They live at the edge of town, not far from the end of the streetcar line. D wasn't there. I left her the following news: "Contessa will be at the end of the line at two p.m."

Around one o'clock, I fetched Contessa from Arnold's. He was cuddling with Mischka. Kissing seems to help his stuttering. Then I rode to the end of the line on the street-car. The closer we got to the end, the more restless Contessa became.

At last we got there.

D didn't see me coming; she was looking in the opposite direction. But Contessa must have smelled D from at least a hundred meters away. She pulled on the leash, and so I let her go. With lots of barking, she ran to D. D turned around, and Contessa leaped up on her. D bent down to Contessa, and Contessa's red fur mixed with D's red hair. I stood apart for a bit. After a while, the two of them had calmed down, and D looked up from her dog's coat. "Did you have her all this time?" she asked, with a sharp edge to her voice.

"No. What do you think? I've had her precisely from one o'clock until now. Arnold had her."

"Arnold? How did he get hold of my Contessa?"

"He bought her off the Internet. But I wrote you all this in the letter."

"I didn't get any letter."

"Contessa's now called Daisy."

"You used to think *my* name was Daisy."

"Yeah, just like I used to think your name could be Danielle, Dorothy, Destiny, Dragana, Dulcinea, Desdemona, Daphne, Diana, or Darcy."

"Or Doris, Dorit, or Dolly."

"But the first name I said was Dagmar."

"Dagmar's crap. Everything's crap."

D was wearing her red nylon sweatpants with the snaps on them. Those sweatpants meant danger. When D's wearing those pants, the world's about to end. She was wearing a tube top, and she had a tattoo around her belly button—intertwined vines. You can get those fake tattoos at the arcade. It had already worn off a bit.

"I'm sorry about that stuff with your mother," I said.

"What do you know about my mother? Have you been spying on me?"

"No."

"Then how do you know? . . . Anyway, there's absolutely nothing wrong with my mother."

"Oh yeah?"

"Yeah."

D bent down over Contessa again and stroked her coat. She could at least have said thank you.

"Where's Sheryl?" I asked, and so immediately put my foot in it.

"Sheryl? She's with her father. And I'm here because of that asshole. He only wanted Sheryl, not me."

"And where's *your* father?"

"My father died a couple of days ago. He had cancer."

"Oh." I didn't believe a word of it.

"As you can see, I've got other things to think about right now."

"Shall we go for a little walk?" I asked.

"I can't be long. My aunt said I had to be back at three."

"Then just for a bit."

Just beyond the end of the line, the city forest begins. The forest is gigantic; it goes on and on. There are paths that crisscross it for kilometers. People are always being told to keep their eyes peeled and remember where their paths turned, especially when they head back, because all the paths look alike.

We walked silently along the stony path. It was cool in the woods. It smelled faintly of mushrooms, and a little like compost. You're not supposed to leave the path, because the forest is threaded by lots of little streams and the ground is boggy.

We walked for more than a little while. But I didn't dare look at my watch. I could only tell that we had walked longer than the short hour we were supposed to have taken. At every fork in the path, I did my best to mark whether we'd followed the right or left path. The woods were getting darker and darker, and the sun had disappeared, although it was probably still shining somewhere. D was getting goose pimples, but we kept going.

Finally we arrived at a clearing. At once the sun came back out and made a fiery halo out of D's hair. There was a little lake in front of us. A couple of crickets were chirping, and from very far away you could hear the sound of the highway. I'd never been there before, and even D seemed to be surprised. The sun hid itself again, and there wasn't a breath of wind. We went down to the shore. There was a sign: Private property. No trespassing! No swimming!

D stuck her hand in the water. "It's warm as a bathtub." Little insects went skittering over the surface of the lake. "I've got to go swimming," D said, and took off her sweatpants. In just her T-shirt and panties, she went clambering over the moss-covered rocks and into the water. "C'mon!"

"It says no swimming here," I said.

"But there's no one around."

I find swampy lakes a bit disgusting. You never know what kind of animals you're going to find living in that kind of water. Leeches? Biting pikes? I recently read in the newspaper about a snapping turtle. Someone brought it back from the Mississippi delta but then released it because it had gotten too big. The turtle lived for ten years in the lake and fed off rats and whole fishes. They captured it before it could bite off anyone's arm.

But then I took off my pants and followed D in. Contessa paddled excitedly alongside us. We swam across the whole lake to a stone pier. There we climbed out of the lake and lay on the stones to dry off.

"I'm not going back to my stupid relatives. They're really mean. I can't do anything, and at night we've got to pray at the table. Can you imagine? My aunt murmurs, 'Come dear Jesus, be our guest' out loud, and after the prayer we've all got to hold hands and say amen. Out loud and like we mean it. Once, I started in to eating first and they slapped my hand. I'm not kidding; it's that uptight. I'm not going to last one more day."

"But where will you go? You can't just take off."

"Sure I can."

"Where will you go?"

"I'll stay here in the forest."

"And what'll you eat?"

"Berries and roots. There are enough around. And I'll go out hunting with Contessa. When it's winter, you can bring me something from time to time."

"The police will have found you long before that. Running away never solves anything."

"Listen, Victor, in all my life I've never met a guy as cowardly as you."

I was sore as hell. D was scratching the nail polish off her left big toe.

"You're a coward too. Writing anonymous letters is also cowardly," I said.

"Hunh."

"What was *that* all about?"

"It's got nothing to do with you."

"But I got some of them all the same."

"It still doesn't have anything to do with you."

"Listen to me; I'll help you if you tell me what was going on with all those letters." By that point, D was scratching off the nail polish on her right big toe. "Were you bored?" D was silent. "Did you want to feel more important?" D put her head down between her arms. "It was all pretty obvious, you know. Because of the secrecy. Any child could have figured it out, what the black three, the red animal, and Asset-noc meant." D started cracking her knuckles. I couldn't think of anything else. I was getting furious. "I'm going now," I said, and stood up.

D said, "Yeah, go."

So I got more furious at that, and I stomped off through the weeds around the lake until I got to where we had left our clothes. I put on my pants and headed off in the direction of the woods. The woods were darker than before and the path even rockier. I didn't get very far because I didn't know the way anymore. Besides, I didn't want to go without D. So I sat down on a fallen tree trunk, wrote all this down, and am hoping that D will turn up. Because if I go any further, I'll get hopelessly lost, and then I'll never see D again, ever.

6:21 p.m. D hasn't shown up. She is the most pig-headed person I know. I'm going back up to the landing. We still have time to find our way out of these woods before dark.

10:52 p.m. Seventy-six degrees. I have forty-seven mosquito bites! When I got back to the landing, D was still sitting there with Contessa. I sat down beside them, and we were quiet. I kept thinking how I was going to convince her to leave the woods before darkness fell, but to everything I said, D only answered, "Hmmm." It was useless. I was once again that stupid Victor.

Suddenly, Contessa began sniffing. First just a bit, then more and more, and that was followed by quiet growling, which quickly grew into something louder. "Someone's coming." D sprang up. While I was gone, she had put on the sweatpants and T-shirt she'd left on the shore. Still, she had goose bumps. The shadows of the trees had lengthened, and the air over the lake was cooling off. Mosquitoes were everywhere. With Contessa collared, D ran along the landing and hid in the bushes, and I followed behind her. Contessa kept growling more and more loudly. When she started to bark, D held her muzzle and whispered, *"Shhhh."* A man was approaching. He had a bag with him, and a rifle. And he was leading a gigantic animal by a leash. Contessa was getting very restless. Even I could smell the strange animal. Then Contessa broke away and sprang out of the bushes. D went after her. She grabbed on to the leash again and dragged Contessa away from the giant dog, and ran off toward the forest.

I'd stayed sitting in the bushes. The man with the rifle said, "Keep quiet, Joseph, it's only children." At that, I also ran away from there. I overtook D at the edge of the woods. D ran on further into the woods. "Get away from here," she cried, "just get away from here!" With which I was in complete agreement. At the fork in the path where I had gotten confused, D took the left path. "Is that the right one?" I asked, panting. I had a stitch in my side. D seemed to be in super shape. "Why are you asking me? Contessa knows the way." So we went on running through the forest, always following Contessa. I didn't understand at all why D was rushing so; the danger was long past and also hadn't been very great. "Why so fast?"

"Can't you run anymore?"

"Yeah, of course."

"Then, run."

At some point, even D was out of breath. We walked the rest of the way back. As usual, the way back was much quicker than the way going had been. It was almost nine o'clock. We were standing in front of her relatives' house. The garden gate was ajar. "See, you didn't buzz off after all," I said.

"It's not so great in the forest, either."

"How did you reach that conclusion?"

"You're alone in the forest. I don't want to be all alone."

"But we're back too late," I said.

"No, I'm not."

"Weren't you supposed to be back at three o'clock?"

"No. That was a lie. My relatives aren't even home. They won't get home until after nine." D was stroking Contessa.

At which point it occurred to me that we still had a bit of a problem, and I asked, "And what'll we do with Contessa?"

"I'll take her with me."

"Listen. That's not going to work. I've got to take her back to Arnold."

"What? I thought you were bringing her back to me."

"Just for today."

"She belongs to me."

"I know that. But if I come back without Contessa, Arnold'll chop my head off."

D was completely dispirited. "You can't take my Contessa away from me again!"

"But only for today. Or for a few days. Until we've made it clear to Arnold that Contessa is your dog."

"I'm not letting Contessa go!"

"Deborah, I—"

"I'm not Deborah. I'm Dagmar. And you, Victor, are a coward."

I was completely panicked, because I just couldn't go back without Contessa. Arnold would kill me on the spot with one of his tae kwon do chops. I had to think of a solution. At once. And one occurred to me. I said, "Dagmar, I've got a solution. Tonight, you let Contessa go, and tomorrow, you come live with us. We've got a lot of space, and my dad will definitely not mind if you live with us for a while. Isn't that a great idea?"

D wrinkled her forehead.

"Then you won't have to live with your relatives anymore. We don't pray over lunch or dinner, and everybody gets to eat when he wants to."

"And Contessa?"

"We'll get her back tomorrow. Would you even be allowed to keep the dog at your relatives'?"

"Hmmm . . . I don't know. They're so refined. And my aunt's afraid of germs. I practically have to take a bath just to sit on the sofa. And she washed all my clothes and fussed because she said they were full of disgusting dog hair."

"You see? You come to my house. My dad will set things straight with your relatives. Maybe they'll even be glad to get rid of you."

"Okay, good," said D finally. "We'll do it like this: you take Contessa back with you and I'll be there tomorrow."

D patted Contessa and gave me back the leash. "Look after her." D disappeared through the garden gate.

SATURDAY, AUGUST 10

10:47 a.m. As usual, Dad's left his half-eaten baloney sandwich lying around. Contessa's sitting in the backyard. Arnold was pretty upset about how late I got back. He said he didn't want to lose a second dog and that evidently I couldn't be trusted. I could just forget about taking Contessa for walks. I can also forget about D. She's not coming. Dad's standing in the bathroom, shaving. He wants me to go with him to the new apartment. But I can't leave. I told Dad he could surely check out the new apartment without me. To which he said I was apathetic and should get my lazy butt in gear.

"My butt isn't lazy. I just can't leave here today."

"Aha! Is the gentleman expecting a visit from a special lady?"

"You might say that," I retorted.

D called this afternoon. She can't come. She had to mow the lawn. I said, "Then come after the lawn's mown."

"Won't work."

"Why not?"

"Because it won't."

"Well, then, I guess it won't." At least I tried to sound indifferent.

Then she said, "Victor, it really won't work. Don't be upset. Maybe tomorrow."

Her voice sounded all thin. "Okay, then tomorrow. Shall I call you?"

"No, never. I'll call you."

Soon afterward, the telephone rang again. It was Lukas, back from the United States. "Hey, Fictor, you old fart! I'm back home. What's up with our bet?" I hadn't even thought about Lukas. I'd thought he was going to be away longer. "We're all here at the pool. This is your big chance." I hesitated to answer. "Maybe you haven't trained enough," Lukas was saying. "I did too . . . okay, good . . . I'm on my way," I responded.

It suddenly struck me that we hadn't planned for the eventuality of *my* winning the bet. Neither Lukas nor I had even considered the possibility. "And what if I win?"

"What do you mean, if you win?"

"Well, if I jump from the ten-meter platform?"

"Ha ha." I heard laughter and voices in the background.

"Lukas. Stop laughing. What's going on. What're you doing?"

"Ha ha ha."

"Listen: If I jump off the ten-meter platform, then you will swear at the start of school, in front of the whole class, that you'll never call me Fictor again. And if you do, then *you'll* have to kiss Saskia."

"Fictor!" Lukas's voice was drowned out by the hubbub.

Now I'm at the pool. It took a few minutes to get my bearings. Of course everyone is here, as if they'd all arranged it. Bombs Away is stretched out on the right where he always lies. Lukas and a couple of others I don't know are lying on the small grass strip between the pools. They're the ones who count. Saskia's standing at the edge of the pool, holding a little boy by the arm. I've chosen the field on the left side of the pool, and I've laid out my towel here. There are more bushes and trees and the people here are for the most part older, families with small children, and those who can't take that much sun. An extremely uncool spot, but you're well hidden. I need some peace and quiet. I've got to get myself together. I've got to plan my strategy. But there's really nothing to plan. It's just got to go quickly. I can't start to think. But I always think. The 10-meter seems scarier and scarier. The 7.5-meter was bad enough. So bad that I've always had the feeling that, okay, this is high enough, but not another centimeter higher. On the other hand, what is the difference? Those silly two and a half meters? That's surely not it; that can't be it. Or is it? Is this what's going to break me?

7.5 meters. I won't get further than that. I've known it all along. From the time I was standing up there with D and she was telling me that it's exactly the same with the 10-meter platform. It's not the same. On the 7.5-meter platform, you're still protected by the posts holding up the 10-meter platform, and also by the ladder going up. And you even have a roof of sorts. Up on the 10-meter platform, there's no roof and the wind whistles. Everything's tiny, and the tower sways from time to time. The water's no longer water, just a faraway turquoise surface that you don't know for sure you can survive smashing into.

I just cannot think anymore. Otherwise I'll never jump. I've been lying here more than half an hour, feeling demoralized. To say nothing of the fact that my journal will soon be full. It just can't end on a bad note. And what was it I was just writing about the end of a movie? The hero jumps from the 10-meter platform, and everyone's watching. And when he emerges from the water, the girl of his dreams is waiting and kisses him. I'm the hero. I'm Victor!

By 5:08 p.m. it was all over. I checked my watch when I jumped. The turquoise surface really was water, and D was right. There's hardly a difference between 7.5 and 10 meters. I did what D always said to do: don't think, go slowly, don't think, don't hesitate. Don't think, and jump. Keep your arms by your sides and make yourself narrow. I jumped, thinking about D as I hit the water.

The water was full of tiny bubbles, and everything around me was turquoise. Without surfacing, I swam in the direction of the ladder. As I was about to climb out of the pool, I saw D standing at the side of the pool, grinning at me. She stretched out her hand and pulled me out. Then she kissed me on the lips. Her lips were cold and wet like mine, and she smelled of peppermint chewing gum.

Stop. Those last five sentences were made up. Of course D wasn't there.

Lukas was pretty shocked, and instead of D, Bombs Away greeted me at the edge of the pool. "You forget what I told you?"

No, I hadn't. And I also had no intention of staying one second more than was necessary. I waved once again at Lukas, who was standing with his swimming buddies up on the platform; then I blew a kiss at Saskia and left them all standing there. Saskia gave me the finger. So did Lukas and Bombs Away.

Actually, I should have been glad, but I was neither proud nor happy that I'd jumped from the 10-meter platform and had won the bet. It was all the same to me. I think it's because of D. When I think about her, my heart starts thumping and I'm also sad, because she's not here and I don't know whether she'll come tomorrow, or if she'll ever come. And if she does, then maybe it'll just be because of her dog and not because of me.

11:02 p.m. Dad's signed a lease. We can move in in October. The apartment isn't half the size of this one, but Dad says we'll save big-time.

Around eight o'clock, Arnold and Mischka stopped by and asked if we'd like to go with them to the beer garden. They were inviting us because they had something to celebrate. Dad grilled the two of them, but all Mischka would do was grin. She had a new hairdo. Her gray-brown hair is now carrot red, which isn't exactly what you'd call an improvement. But the style is cool. Arnold was wearing a white shirt.

In the beer garden, Arnold ordered roast pork for everyone.

"Now, would you finally tell us what you're celebrating?" demanded Dad.

"We've gotten engaged," said Arnold without a bit of stuttering, and Mischka grinned broadly with her crooked teeth. "And," she added, "Arnold's given notice on his apartment. We'll be living in my place from now on."

"That way, we'll save on rent," Arnold added. "G-g-good, n-n-no?"

Dad and I thought the stuff about the rent was very impressive, and we congratulated them on their engagement. "We want to have four children," explained Mischka.

"What about your plants?" Dad asked.

"Plants and children aren't mutually exclusive," Mischka said. "Both are living things that have to be treated with love."

Dad laughed. "And if the kids get on your nerves, you can throw them to your carnivorous plants."

"Paul!" said Mischka.

Dad and I looked at each other and had to grin. I'm sure Dad was thinking the same thing I was: stuttering kiddies who'll get tae kwon do lessons every day and have to go to church on Sundays. Then the beer arrived. Although Mischka was against it, I got one too. Arnold and Mischka got all happy with the beer. I just got tired, and Dad got melancholy. "And we're just two sad sacks, aren't we, Victor?" I was nodding, because I was feeling that way, even though I hadn't the faintest idea how Dad got the impression I could be sad. I was stroking Contessa, who was lying beneath the table at my feet. She didn't even want to taste my roast pork, she was so unhappy because D wasn't there. Then I started looking around at the other patrons. "Look over there! There's Edda!" I whispered to Dad.

"Edda," said Dad, somberly.

"Edda?" asked Mischka, shrilly.

"*Shhhhh* . . . I absolutely don't want to see her," whispered Dad, although he still craned his neck to look over. "She's doubled!" he said, astounded.

"Of course," I answered. "She's got a twin sister."

Dad was shaking his head. "That's way too much for me."

Edda and her sister sat down a couple of tables away and raised their beer glasses to drink. Mischka sprang up. "We've got to say hello and ask how she's doing."

"No, we don't," grunted Dad. He wasn't thrilled by Mischka's enthusiasm.

"It looks as though she's doing better," Mischka said.

"Was she ill?" I asked.

"She was depressed, her sister said."

"I'm depressed too," Dad said.

"Me too," I said, although I didn't exactly know what depression was.

Mischka was finally happy just to wave at Edda.

Arnold and Mischka were drunk and getting the giggles; Dad was also tipsy and not saying anything. "At least we're getting a new apartment," I said, to try to comfort Dad as well as myself.

Then we left. The stars were shining. Up in the sky, you could see Vega in the Lyre, Deneb in the Swan, and Altair in the Eagle; those stars make up a triangle you can see best during the summer. Tomorrow, we'll be able to see the Perseids. There are shooting stars everywhere that fall from the sky then, and you can wish on them. Tomorrow is D's birthday.

I looked up depression in the medical reference book that Dad has. *Depress, depression (to press downward):... Psychiatric: ill humor; sad ill humor.*

SUNDAY, AUGUST 11

In my desk drawer, I found a roll of wrapping paper and wrapped the Nikes in it. For D, in case she comes over. I think they'll suit her. Then I tidied up my room and threw away all the anonymous letters. The gifts from Mom, at least the ones that Sheryl hadn't destroyed, I put back on the shelves. There they are then, unwanted. But they always were.

In the meantime, it's become afternoon, and I'm no longer sure whether or not I want D to come and stay. What if Dad is against it? I didn't even ask him. Maybe he won't want to have D stay here. And her relatives will probably have something to say about it. It was silly to promise D she could come live here.

There's only one page left in the book. But that's fine with me. I don't have any desire to write more.

* * *

Dad was in the kitchen and tossed me a letter. "Mom wrote!"

"Did mail come today?"

"No, yesterday. I forgot to give you the letter."

I tore open the envelope. There was a postcard inside, of a lady diver diving from a platform straight as a knife into the water. The water was shining turquoise; the diver had red hair. I'd have liked to shred that postcard. Mom had written on a sheet of light blue stationery that was folded inside the envelope:

> *Dear Victor,*
>
> *Don't be angry that I've gone off again without saying goodbye to you. I had to go, because everything here is moving too fast for me and I need time to think it all over. That's the reason I've booked a flight to Canada, and by the time you read this letter, I'll already be in the air.*
>
> *I did invite you to spend some of your summer here with me, but that won't happen now, unfortunately. At any rate, I got the impression that you are pretty busy and didn't need*

my invitation. You're already big, now; I forget that sometimes, and I also forget that you might possibly find it a bit dull to sit around here out in the country and play tractor with the neighbor kids.

At any rate, when I get back from Canada, I'm going to look for an apartment in town near you and Dad; first, because living in the country has gotten boring for me, too, and secondly because I've realized how little I know about you and how little time I've had to spend with you.

Well, now I've got to pack; I'm leaving tonight.

Tell Dad hi for me.

With love,

Mom

Mom. I could also have shredded that letter. Mom can rot in Canada for all I care.

"What's she say?" asked Dad over my shoulder. I gave him the letter. Dad read it and said, "Women!" and gave it back to me.

"What do you think she'll bring me from Canada?" I asked.

"Don't know. Maybe maple syrup. Or a bearskin." He sighed.

Now Dad's in the kitchen making spaghetti with tomato sauce. You know, I'm actually finding it pretty nice that Mom is going to move here after her vacation. Maybe she really will come back again. I mean for real. Even if it takes a little time. You've got to be patient with adults. Half the time they don't know what they want. Dad's hollering from the kitchen, "Victor, can you get the door? Someone's ringing!"

11:09 p.m. Sum total: 11. I've had to glue a couple of extra pages into my diary. It was D standing at our front door. She was completely at loose ends, and it was all she could do to stammer, "I—I just can't take it anymore." She stumbled by me into the apartment and ran directly into the kitchen, where Dad was getting ready to test his spaghetti. She didn't seem to notice Dad at all and just sat down in Mom's place and buried her head in her arms. She was crying. I stood in the kitchen doorway, and it all felt dreadfully uncomfortable. Actually, I should have felt truly sorry for D, since she was the very picture of misery, but it only embarrassed me. In front of Dad. Besides that, I hadn't the faintest idea what I should do. D raised her head. "Where's Contessa?"

"Upstairs."

"I want her back."

"Who is Contessa?" asked Dad.

"Daisy," I explained.

"It's not Daisy, it's Contessa, and Contessa is mine. She's mine and no one else's."

"Arnold's new dog?" asked Dad.

"Yes," I said, and added quickly, "but she's actually Deborah's dog."

"I'm not Deborah, I'm Dagmar."

"Daisy, Dagmar, Deborah, Contessa. It's like I said, 'Women'!"

"Dad. Would you please stay out of it?"

"Now, look; there's a girl I don't know sitting in my kitchen in that chair. She's either named Deborah or Dagmar, and she believes she possesses a dog that is named either Daisy or Contessa. And you want me to stay out of it?"

"Why don't you cook the spaghetti?" I said, and took D's hand and pulled her out of the kitchen. Her hand was cold as ice. Her face was all swollen; she'd probably been crying the whole day. I sat her down on my bed, where she let herself fall onto her side and pulled the covers up over herself, although it was humid and warm. I sat down beside her and didn't know what I should say.

Suddenly, she surfaced from under the covers, shook her hair out, and said, "What's up? Can I live with you? And when can we go get Contessa?"

"I haven't asked Dad."

"What? You haven't asked? But you've had two whole days."

I was silent.

"Victor, I thought it was all arranged."

"Nothing was all arranged. I only said maybe. If it was all right with Dad."

"You didn't even ask."

"I was thinking . . . ," I said.

"I'm not interested in what you're thinking. What you're thinking isn't important; it's what you're doing."

That's true. I should leave off thinking. Or start thinking *clearly*. No more half-baked stuff. And so I said, "We'll talk with my dad. I'm sure he won't object." I wasn't all that sure about it. At that moment, there was a knock on my door. Dad said supper was ready and asked whether or not we'd have the courtesy to come and dine with an older gentleman.

So we went into the kitchen and sat down at the table, which Dad had set. Usually, no one sets the table at our place; everyone gets what he needs from the cupboard. But then again, we almost never eat together either.

Dad dished out gigantic portions. D picked at the food, and I thought about just how I should begin. But it was Dad who spoke first. "Doesn't it taste good?" D was shrugging.

"Why were you crying so hard earlier?" Dad asked.

D answered after a long silence. "Because my dog's at that Arnold's, and . . ."

". . . and D's got to live with these relatives who she can't stand and who don't like dogs," I said.

"Why are you living with relatives?" Dad wanted to know.

"My mom's in the hospital."

"For a long time?"

"Yes. Maybe."

I took a deep breath. It was finally time for me to speak. "Dad . . . listen . . . can Dagmar live with us?" Dad's fork halted on the way to his mouth. "I mean, just for a while, until her mother's well again," I added.

Dad wasn't getting it. "Who is Dagmar?"

"Me."

"I thought you were Deborah."

"No, I'm Dagmar."

Dad put down his fork and wiped his mouth. "Kids, do you really think it's that easy? It won't work."

"But, Dad . . ."

"Look, it doesn't matter to me. As far as I'm concerned, the whole world can live here. But Daisy can't just move in here."

"Daisy?"

"Er . . . Dagborah. Or whatever her name is. Where she lives is up to the juvenile court. Or her relatives. I don't have a thing to say about it. I'm not home at night, and I sleep half the day; nobody cooks regularly as a rule, and there's no woman in the house."

"But I live with you."

"That's different."

"What's different about it?"

"We're related. I'm your father."

D was shifting around uneasily at her place. "Great, Victor, just great," she said. "First you make big promises, and then you don't keep them. Well, I guess I'll just go." She stood up.

"Dagmar! Stay here, maybe we'll come up with another solution," Dad said.

"There isn't any," D said, and was already going out the door. I followed and caught up to her in the hallway. There isn't any solution, I was thinking. But only for a moment, because then I saw it. Through the hall window, you can see down into the backyard. Contessa was sitting there. I said to D, "Give me just five minutes. Then you can do whatever you want."

I didn't wait for her answer but instead ran past her out of the building and down into the backyard. I wanted to get Contessa. I couldn't have cared less about Arnold. I'd have to explain it to him another time. No sooner was I down in the backyard than Contessa ran up to me, waggling excitedly. I'm sure she could smell D on me. I nabbed her by the collar and went back up the stairs with her. At the door, she broke away and raced down the hall, barking.

"Contessa!" shrieked D, and the two merged into a red-haired tangle.

"I've got to get ready to go to work," Dad broke in, "but if you want, I'll take Dagmar back to her relatives. Maybe I can talk with them. I have an idea."

D wasn't listening, she was so absorbed in Contessa.

"I've been thinking we might go away, the two of us, Victor, at the end of the summer, for a bit. As far as I'm concerned, the three of us could go. Or even the four of us, if it comes to that, with the mutt."

"Did you hear that?" I asked D.

"What?" She raised her head.

Dad explained everything again.

"But what'll I do with Contessa now? And tomorrow? And the day after tomorrow?" D asked. Her voice was sounding a bit more hopeful than it had earlier.

"Maybe your relatives aren't as bad as all that. At any rate, I'll talk with them."

We climbed into Dad's taxi and drove off. In the car, I presented my gift to D. "You're the only one who remembered my birthday," she said, misty-eyed. "Besides, I've never been in a taxi before."

Dad pulled up outside the house of D's relatives. D was trembling a little, and I took her hand. Together, we all went in through the little garden gate, Dad first and Contessa snuffling along behind.

The door of the house was painted blue, and the name Ochmann was on a wooden sign painted with flowers. Dad straightened out his shirt after he had rung the doorbell. A woman opened the door. She had the same hair as D and the same color eyes. I'd imagined the aunt as some kind of dragon, but she looked just like an ordinary human being. Dad greeted her politely and introduced himself. The aunt eyed Dad up and down and invited us in. She threw a sharp glance at Contessa. I was thinking, This could be amusing.

We walked through a dark hall with brown floral wallpaper. It smelled of sour pickles. In the dining room, which had an orange floral carpet, we sat down at a table. In a row along the windowsills were countless cactuses. The aunt interrupted Dad, who had been talking a blue streak: "All right, what exactly is this all about?" To Dagmar, she said, "Please take that dog into the garden. The whole place will be full of hair." Dad took a breath. And I held mine. Here's the upshot of our negotiations:

1. Contessa can stay with the relatives.

2. But she's got to sleep in the shed. Because of the hair.

3. D can go away with us.

4. But not out of the country.

Now, yet again, I won't get to go out of the country, even though Dad had mentioned something about Italy. But that doesn't matter.

Dad carried on talking with the aunt for a while, about rental housing, school problems, and the raising of cactuses. I was more and more astounded at Dad; I hadn't thought he could be so polite. D nodded at me, and we went into the garden. "But don't let that dog get into the vegetable garden."

D was rolling her eyes. "She's like that all the time."

"During the day you can come visit us," I said. We were inspecting the shed, Contessa's designated sleeping quarters. The evening was already growing dusky.

Dad came out onto the patio with the aunt. "I've got to get going," he said. It was eight o'clock. "Do you want to stay here a bit longer, Victor?" he asked. I nodded.

"Okay. But at eleven, you're to be back home. And in bed."

"Yeah, yeah."

"I mean it. You know I've got eyes in the back of my head." In front of D's aunt, Dad was coming on as stricter than he really is. "And say hi to the Perseids for me." He turned away and shook the aunt's hand. Then he disappeared. I heard the engine, and then Dad briefly beeping his horn.

"Who are you supposed to say hi to?" D asked me.

"The Perseids. You can see a whole lot of shooting stars today, because the earth is passing through a meteor shower. Did you know that shooting stars are really tiny? No larger than particles of dust?"

D was looking up now too. "I don't see any."

"It's not really dark yet."

"If you see a shooting star, you can wish on it, can't you?" D asked. "You know what? I'll show you a place where we can see the sky much better. Then we can make a lot of wishes." She took me by the hand and we walked down the street a way, until we came to a small hill. We climbed up. There was a playground at the top with sandboxes, seesaws, and swings. We let Contessa off the leash and began swinging. In the meantime, it had grown almost dark.

"Where is Sirius?" D asked suddenly.

"You can't see it right now. You can only see it in winter."

"And why is it called the dog star?"

"Because it's in the constellation Canis Major," I explained. D was silent. I went on, "Hey, listen, do you think it has any influence? It's the dog days, and suddenly everything that's been going on has to do with dogs. They die, they're abducted, they return. Heaven only knows what else is going to happen."

D didn't answer. She was swinging higher and higher, and then she jumped off and landed in the sand and disappeared into the dark. "Dagmar," I shouted, stopping my swing and running after her.

The grass was cool and wet with dew. D was standing by a bush. She looked at me and her eyes were brimming. She was crying. "I think everything is my fault. Maybe Arnold should keep Contessa. I'm so horrible." D snuffled.

"What are you talking about? Contessa's your dog," I said, and I put my arm around her shoulder.

"Sure. But I took his away from him."

"What?"

Now D was sobbing for real. She couldn't pull herself together. "It was all such a good idea. I wanted to be a dog breeder. Contessa is purebred, and there aren't all that many purebred red male cocker spaniels in town. And one day, I happened to see Kaiser Wilhelm. Every day he sat out there in that backyard, getting more and more bored. I thought I'd bring the two of them together. Contessa and Kaiser Wilhelm. I wanted lots of little puppies. What do you think a pedigreed cocker spaniel like that is worth?"

"How did you know Kaiser Wilhelm was pedigreed?"

"Oh, cut it out."

"Don't lie to me. You must have been in Arnold's apartment before. That's why you have the same key chain as I do, that one with the close parentheses, x, open parentheses belly button."

"He's got a whole drawer of them. I was sure he wouldn't miss just one."

"And why were you in Edda's apartment?"

"The door was open. Her twin sister was taking her away. She was completely spaced out and kept babbling about aliens and Sirius. Just sheer nonsense. I couldn't help being curious. I've been at your place too. And at Mischka's as well."

"At our place? How did you get in?"

"Oh, well. Through the door. You can pick the lock with a telephone calling card. You can pick every door in your building with one."

"But why were you snooping around there at all?"

"I just wanted to know who was living in such a great building. In such big apartments. With such high ceilings. Your building is like a castle, and when I was in your apartments, I got to feeling a little bit like I was living there too. Sometimes I stayed the whole afternoon at Mischka's and fed her plants."

"Where do you get off with these ideas?"

"They're completely normal."

"Completely normal? You're off your rocker. That's why you had to go see Grützow."

"How do you know about that?"

"She's got a whole file on you."

"You don't mean to tell me that you read it?"

"Of course I read it."

D was all for bolting at that point, but I grabbed her fast and said, "That won't work. Look, either you tell me everything now, or . . ."

"Or?"

"Or I'll tell Arnold that you've stolen Daisy."

"You're a beast."

"Yeah. So, talk already!" We had gone back to the playground by this point and had sat ourselves down on one of the benches. The benches there are just the same as the ones in Kennedy Square.

"Why were you snooping around Grützow's?" D wanted to know.

"You break into strangers' apartments, and so do I. Anyway, I don't care that you're going to see Grützow. My dad said I should be going there as well."

"But you don't *have* to go. That's the difference."

Yes, that was a difference.

"Then you know everything about me."

"Only what Grützow had written down. For instance, when your birthday is. That's really not such a big deal." By mistake, I knocked D's side with my elbow. "And now, tell me what was up with Kaiser Wilhelm?"

"He didn't want to have anything to do with my Contessa. That's why I fed him the vitamin pills. I thought they were going to make him more energetic. That was on July twenty-third. And the next day he was dead. The stupidest thing, though, was that Arnold had seen me in the backyard with Kaiser Wilhelm. That's the reason I started writing the letters in the first place. I was thinking I could throw suspicion off me and onto someone else in the building. Besides, I thought it wasn't fair that all of you lived in such a beautiful building and I had to live in such a tiny hole. If only you guys would at least furnish your apartments properly! But you leave them half empty, or make foolish martial arts studios out of them, or turn them into greenhouses! I figured you guys deserved the letters."

"You brought Edda to the edge of a nervous breakdown, and everyone suspected me for a while."

All D could do was giggle. "You?"

"Stop laughing! Did you think up the letters yourself?"

"Only half. I discovered ones like them on the Internet. I just changed them a little, so that they'd fit you and your building."

"And all that drama about the numbers. What's the significance of eleven, for instance?"

"I just like the number. It's pretty when it's doubled. And my birthday's the eleventh. What else?"

"Why did you call yourself Deborah?"

"I hate the name Dagmar. And it's nice to have a lot of names when you don't have anything else."

I sat thinking about all of it for a while, but it was as if my brain had gone fuzzy because D was sitting next to me and she was all warm.

"A vitamin pill couldn't kill a dog," I said, and took D's hand.

"No?"

"No way. Kaiser Wilhelm was sitting down there in that backyard all the time, and he must have eaten something out of the garbage. Who knows what was in there? Maybe the owner has something against dogs."

"You don't think the vitamin pills were to blame?"

"Not a chance."

D exhaled.

I had decided I was going to kiss D as soon as I saw a shooting star. The shooting star appeared at 9:02 p.m. Sum total: 11.

Martina Wildner is a freelance artist and writer. She lives in Germany.